finally,
SOMETHING DANGEROUS
THE ONE AND ONLYS AND THE CASE OF THE ROBOT CROW

Also by Doug Cornett

Finally, Something Mysterious

DOUG CORNETT

→finally,←
SOMETHING DANGEROUS
THE ONE AND ONLYS AND THE CASE OF THE ROBOT CROW

THE ONE AND ONLYS

2

ALFRED A. KNOPF • NEW YORK

THIS IS A BORZOI BOOK PUBLISHED BY ALFRED A. KNOPF

Visit us on the Web! rhcbooks.com

Educators and librarians, for a variety of teaching tools, visit us at RHTeachersLibrarians.com

Library of Congress Cataloging-in-Publication Data
Names: Cornett, Doug, author.
Title: Finally, something dangerous: the One and Onlys and the Case of the Robot Crow / Doug Cornett.
Description: First edition. | New York: Alfred A. Knopf Books for Young Readers, 2022. | Series: The One and Onlys; 2 | Audience: Ages 8–12. | Audience: Grades 7–9. | Summary: Bellwood's finest kid detective team sets out to discover who is controlling the robot crows that are showing up around town.
Identifiers: LCCN 2021042135 (print) | LCCN 2021042136 (ebook) | ISBN 978-0-593-43292-1 (hardcover) | ISBN 978-0-593-43293-8 (lib. bdg.) | ISBN 978-0-593-43294-5 (ebook)
Subjects: CYAC: Mystery and detective stories. | LCGFT: Novels. | Detective and mystery fiction.
Classification: LCC PZ7.1.C6728 Fg 2022 (print) | LCC PZ7.1.C6728 (ebook) | DDC [Fic]—dc23

The text of this book is set in 12-point Bell MT Pro.

Printed in the United States of America
10 9 8 7 6 5 4 3 2 1
First Edition

» To Leo, Anna, and Althea «

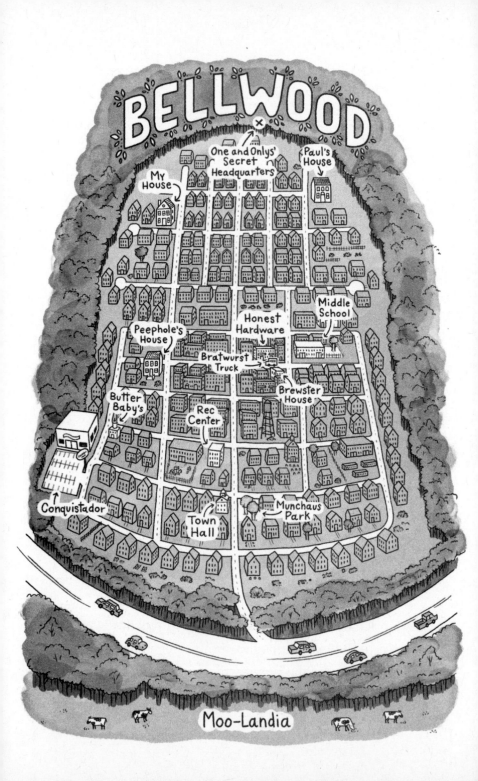

⇒ 1 ⇐

Welcome to New Bellwood

I should have known something strange was going on when I first saw the crows arguing in my front yard. I'd just stepped out the door, ready to hop on my bike and zip across town to Bellwood Middle School for my first day of sixth grade, when I heard all the noise. *Squonk! Squonk! Squonk!* they went, a pair of black birds on the grass, letting a third crow in a tree really have it. I didn't have to speak bird language to know that those two were not happy. It was all *squonk* this and *squonk* that as they shifted menacingly on their feet and ruffled their feathers. But the crow up in the tree didn't seem to mind. It just sat there, unmoving. There was something admirable about the way it was completely in its own world.

Little did I know that by that afternoon I'd be plunged into the Case of the Robot Crow, which would turn out to be a battle for the very soul of Bellwood, our weird little nowhere town. The world-famous detective trio the One and Onlys—me (my full name is Gloria Long-shanks Hill, but everyone calls me Shanks) and my best friends, Paul and Peephole (real name Alexander, but only his parents and teachers call him that)—were still celebrating solving our greatest case yet, which had involved some mysterious rubber duckies that showed up in Bellwood, when an even stranger, even more dangerous problem fell into our laps.

"Shanks!" My dad's voice drifted out from the kitchen window. "You better get a move on. It's bad luck to be late for the first day of school!"

"I don't believe in luck, Dad," I said, hopping onto my bike. I gave a nod to the bird up in the tree, sniffed the peculiarly sweet air, and pushed my bike out into the road.

The first day of sixth grade was a sloppy hurricane of crowded hallways, weird middle-school body odor, cafeteria crinkle fries smushed into the soles of everyone's sneakers, and an impossible labyrinth of classrooms. All the kids skittered around, showing off their first-day-of-school clothes and congratulating each other on getting so much taller. Well, I hadn't gotten any taller, but do you think that bothered me? Not at all. I had no problem being pretty much the shortest person in the whole middle school. But it was a good idea to never mention it to my face.

Maybe it's a middle-school thing, but every teacher

seemed to have one pet peeve they absolutely would not tolerate in their class. For Mrs. Nguyen, it was the sound of paper being ripped out of a notebook. For Mr. Gormski, it was the smell of energy drinks. If you wore a hat in Mr. McClelland's class, you might as well bring your signed last will and testament. But as far as I could tell, our social studies teacher, Mrs. Espinoza, was super chill. She spoke in a calm, even voice, and she moved across the room slowly and deliberately, like she was carefully wading through ankle-deep water. She didn't even get mad at Peephole, Paul, and me for squealing with delight when we saw that we were all in the same class.

But then Mrs. Espinoza laid it on us. She was giving us homework on the very first day. And not just homework, but a major project. Bellwood didn't have only one story of its past, she said. Instead, it had countless stories, each featuring different people. To get to know the many stories of Bellwood's past, each of us was to choose a building in town, research its history, and then make a five-minute presentation of our findings to the class. And we had only two weeks to do it.

The bell rang to signal the end of class, and Peephole let out a groan. He was pale and looked a little nauseous.

"You okay, dude?" I asked, stuffing my books into my bag and flinging it over my back. "You look like somebody died."

"Somebody did die," he said. "My free time. And what if I can't decide on a building to research? What if I pick a place but somebody else picks it, too, and then their presentation is better? What if I pick a place but it has no history at all? I'm so scared."

"Don't worry, Peephole," Paul said, giving him a supportive slap on the back. "We'll help you find a good place."

Being scared of homework might sound weird, but only if you didn't know Peephole. See, he was pretty much the opposite of me. My parents liked to say I was born without two things: hair and fear. I eventually grew hair. Long, electric-blond hair that cascaded all the way down my back. But fear never sprouted. Peephole, on the other hand, was afraid of . . . well, everything. You know how people joke about somebody being afraid of their own shadow? I've seen Peephole get so startled by his shadow that he literally shrieked. More than once. But I had to give him credit: he'd done a lot of growing up ever since he became a big brother over the summer. He was eleven years older than his sister, so he was a *really* big brother. His baby sister, tiny Trillium, forced Peephole to become a little bit braver. Just a little bit.

That also meant that he was no longer an only child like Paul and me, which made our detective team name, the One and Onlys, sort of not true. But it was such a good name that we decided to ignore that detail.

The three of us spilled out of the classroom into the crowded hallway, where we joined the herd being corralled toward the gym for an assembly.

"Hey, wasn't there a fire at the Bellwood Library a long time ago?" I asked. A seed of an idea was forming in my head.

"I think so," Paul said. "The place nearly burned down back in the eighties, when our parents were kids. Why?"

"Picture this," I said, jumping ahead and walking backward to face them. "The presentation starts with the lights off. A spotlight flips on, and you see a perfect scale model of the library on a table at the front of the classroom. There's a voice—it's me—explaining the boring history of the building, that it was built in blah-blah by blah, but suddenly, *whuuffff*, the library bursts into flames!"

"You can't have a fire in the classroom!" Peephole gasped.

"Sure I can." I shrugged. "I'll be crouched behind the model with a blowtorch. So the library lights up like a sparkler on the Fourth of July, and I throw some siren sound effects in there, and then, just when everybody starts freaking out, I jump up and extinguish the flames. Mrs. Espinoza is so dazzled by the whole thing, she gives the project an A-plus right then and there."

"I like the enthusiasm," Paul said. "But I'm not sure if Mrs. Espinoza is going to allow real flames." Of the three One and Onlys, Paul was the voice of reason. He was so level-headed that you could balance your lunch tray on his noggin and never worry about it spilling. It was hard to get Paul angry or worked up or emotional about anything, except for mysteries, of course. He was an absolute nut for them. He loved hunting them out, investigating them, and solving them.

When we finally reached the doors of the gym, our math teacher, Mr. McClelland, was plucking hats off kids' heads and directing them to the bleachers.

"Find your seats quickly," he said as we passed by. "We have a special guest speaker today."

Sure enough, standing at a microphone in the middle of the basketball court was Bellwood's mayor, Frank Pilkington, who had a tradition of visiting schools on the first day. Tall and wiry, with a fountain of blond hair bursting up and out from his head, Mayor Pilkington was the town's jack-in-the-box: you never knew when he was going to pop up. He flashed a wide grin at the buzzing throng of students, patiently clasping his hands in front of him.

"How about you, Paul?" I asked as we climbed the bleachers to our perch at the top. "That sharp mind of yours come up with any ideas for the history project?"

"My parents' hardware store has been in the family for three generations," he said, nodding. "I've always wanted to learn more about the store's history."

"That *is* a cool idea," Peephole said. "What if I can't find a cool idea, too? What if I forget about the project altogether and end up getting an F? What if instead of giving a presentation, I just go up to the front of the class and barf?"

"We'll help clean it up," Paul said.

"Totally," I agreed. "After I take a picture of it for memory's sake."

A hush fell over the crowd as our principal, Mrs. Samuels, held her hands up in the quiet coyote gesture—otherwise known as the be-quiet-right-now-or-else pose. She motioned for Mayor Pilkington to begin speaking, and he did. At least, I think he did. His lips were moving, and he seemed to be laughing at his own joke, but no sound was coming through the speakers.

"Turn the mic on!" somebody yelled. And then everybody yelled it.

A smartly dressed woman with black hair down to her shoulders quickly trotted over to Mayor Pilkington, the click of her high heels echoing up to our ears. I recognized her from the Lyrical Warriors Poetry Wrestling Club meetings at the Bellwood Recreation Center that I went to with my parents every Monday and Thursday night. It was Tania Rose, the mayor's assistant. She grasped the mic, flicked a button, then clicked back to her seat.

"Hello, Bellwood Middle School!" Mayor Pilkington boomed into the mic, which responded with a high-pitched hiss. "The first day of school marks a new beginning for you all, and I'd like to talk to you today about another new beginning . . . for *all* of us Bellwoodians. Imagine this." Mayor Pilkington plucked the mic from its stand and took a few steps toward the bleachers. "You've stepped out of a time machine into the Bellwood of the future. It's still the same old Bellwood, the place we all love, the place we all call home, but it's *newer*. The pavement is polished smooth. There are elegant new streetlamps on every corner. Exciting new restaurants offer bold new flavors. New businesses open their doors and invite you in. A bright new home awaits us all. Welcome," Mayor Pilkington announced in a grand voice, a proud grin on his face as he swept his arm across the bleachers filled with middle-school students, "to New Bellwood!"

He held his arms up for a second or two in the silence, and I realized that he was probably waiting for applause. From my seat up in the corner of the bleachers, I clapped loudly, which startled a few other kids and teachers around me into clapping, too. A weak tinkling of applause spread through the packed gym, but Mayor Pilkington seemed satisfied.

The theme for the day's assembly was, you guessed it, New Bellwood, and Mayor Pilkington was giving the same speech I'd already heard several times at meetings of the Lyrical Warriors Poetry Wrestling Club. But even if he'd delivered it a hundred times before, he still radiated optimism. He really meant every word of it. Nobody loved Bellwood more than Mayor Pilkington. But still, there was something a little more urgent in his tone this time around. Maybe even desperate?

"And you, bright youth of Bellwood, don't even need a time machine to travel to New Bellwood. The change is happening right now, as we speak! In a few short weeks, the brand-new library will open its doors. And if you've seen work crews hammering away at the roads or climbing up power lines, you've seen the transformation. If you've heard the *chuk chuk chuk* of the new town-wide sprinkler system or admired the vibrant green grass, you've seen the transformation. If you've basked in the warm glow of the new streetlamps, soon to be on every block in Bellwood, then you've seen the transformation. If your mouth has watered at the thought of the new restaurants popping up in town, you've tasted the transformation. If you've flushed your toilet and admired how efficiently the water swirls into our new sewer system, you've experienced the transformation."

I felt a little bad for Mayor Pilkington. He was clearly jazzed about New Bellwood, but he wasn't getting much reaction from the audience. People in Bellwood tended to like it just the way it was. Also, an assembly of students at the end of a long first day was a tough crowd. From my perch up in the corner, I had a good view of the student body of Bellwood Middle School. I could see a lot of them nodding drowsily, and some were straight-up asleep. Those who were awake were staring at Mayor Pilkington with thinly veiled boredom, holding whispered conversations, or amusing themselves with games. There seemed to be a particularly heated rock-paper-scissors match under way in the opposite bleachers, with two boys slamming their fists into their palms— one-two-three, one-two-three—like the beat of an angry waltz. When I looked closer, I was not surprised to see that it was the twins Jeb and Zeb Beverly, the most competitive kids in town. Some of the teachers were policing the crowd and shushing students, others were scrolling through their phones, and others were shushing students while pretending that they weren't also scrolling through their phones.

"I've got a question for you." Mayor Pilkington's voice drifted up to us from the makeshift stage. He spun around slowly to address all the students in the gym. "What kind of dreams do *you* have for New Bellwood?"

There were a few seconds of silence while we waited for his speech to continue, but it seemed like he actually wanted us to respond. All four hundred of us. Suddenly, he got his wish. The gym erupted into a chaotic chorus of voices shouting different answers.

"A professional baseball team!" shouted the kid in front of me. It was Chad Foster, Bellwood's best trombone player and biggest sports fan.

"A twenty-four-hour all-you-can-eat dinosaur-themed pizza buffet!" a girl a few rows down yelled.

"A disco bowling alley!" hollered a custodian near the doors, and then he seemed embarrassed at how loud his voice was.

As the gym got noisier, the teachers just shook their heads in dismay. They knew that Pilkington had made an amateur blunder: never ask a question to a gymnasium full of students.

"No more school assemblies!" a voice called out rudely. Okay—it was me.

Harmonica Ed, a famous eighth grader down near the front row, pulled his harmonica out of his pocket and started playing. And next to him, as always, was his best friend and shadow, Flyin' Brian Saucer, bobbing his head to the tune.

"Poor guy," I said, looking down at Mayor Pilkington, who was laughing nervously and waving his arms. He was like a person trying to put out a raging inferno by blowing on it.

"He's probably wishing he could go back in time and not ask that question," Peephole said.

"I kind of don't get it," Paul said, biting his lip. "Why is everybody so eager for New Bellwood? I think the old Bellwood was just fine. Why do we need a bunch of new restaurants coming in out of nowhere?"

Ever since the new megastore, the Conquistador, opened in Bellwood last summer, Paul's family's hardware store had been struggling to compete. They opened a bratwurst truck in the parking lot of the hardware store, which quickly became a local favorite, but still, Paul was a little suspicious of new businesses coming in.

"Don't worry, Paul, your folks still make the best bratwurst this town has ever seen." It was true. Last summer, they'd won the Bellwood Bratwurst Bonanza with their special recipe, which made them local celebrities. The Triple B was the biggest and most important party all year. Half the town entered a bratwurst into the competition, and if you won, you were treated like the emperor of Rome. Since Paul's parents had scored a surprise upset victory over Mr. Babbage, the long-standing Bratwurst King of Bellwood, they were now the official Wieners, at least until next year's competition. They had the trophy and the new bratwurst truck to prove it. You haven't lived until you've tasted their pancake-wrapped bratwurst, which they call the Swine in a Sleeping Bag.

"You guys talking about Bellwood history?"

The voice came from nearby. We all turned to see Dorothea Hightower, my next-door neighbor, peeking out, as usual, from behind a thick book. Her black hair was twisted into braids, and her wide, round glasses made her face look narrow. "I find our town's history fascinating, too!"

"Oh, hey, Dorothea," I said. We weren't close friends, but we were friendly neighbors. Every time I saw her, she'd tell me another interesting fact about Bellwood's past.

"Sounds like there's going to be a lot of changes around here," she said. "Exciting, isn't it?"

"It's not all exciting," Paul said grumpily.

Dorothea nodded. "I know what you mean. Change can be a little scary. But as long as we don't forget our past, I think change can be a good thing."

"I guess," Paul said, not quite convinced. "Just seems like Bellwood was perfect to begin with."

"Perfect?" Dorothea's eyebrow arched, and she looked at Paul thoughtfully. Three or four rows down from us, somebody had busted out an acoustic guitar and was leading a sing-along of "Row, Row, Row Your Boat." A few rows farther, some kids were doing jumping jacks. Across the court, Zeb and Jeb had moved on to a full-fledged poker game. Yep, never ask an open-ended question at an assembly.

Dorothea lifted a clipboard off her lap and clutched it to her chest. "So you guys are in Mrs. Espinoza's social studies class, right? Well, I've got a great idea for the history project."

"Seems like everybody does," Peephole said, "except me."

"You know the old Brewster House?" Dorothea asked.

"Sure," Paul said. "It's right across the street from my family's store and our bratwurst truck. It's been in Bellwood forever. It was a hotel once, right?"

Dorothea nodded. "It's been a couple of different things, but it was built as a hotel in 1885. It's sort of falling apart because it hasn't been in use for decades. See, it's an important building in Bellwood's history, and in my family's history, too. My great-grandpa lived at the Brewster House for a short while."

"That must have been a long time ago," I said. "Is he still alive? Could you interview him for your project?"

Dorothea shook her head. "He died before I was born, so I never got to meet him. But I have this." She stretched out her fingers to show a silver ring. "He gave it to my great-grandma when he proposed to her. And now I have it. Isn't that cool?"

"It's still shiny," I said admiringly.

"It's a way of feeling connected to them," Dorothea said. "And to remind me of the way things used to be in Bellwood."

"It's like my parents' store," Paul said, examining Dorothea's ring. "My great-grandpa built it, and it's been passed down through the generations. I'll probably be in charge of it someday, too. That is, if it's still open when I'm an adult."

"I'm sure it will be," Dorothea said. She passed the clipboard to Paul. "I have an idea to turn the Brewster House into a museum of Bellwood's past. I talked to Mayor Pilkington about it a couple of weeks ago. He said if I could get five hundred signatures, he'd pitch the idea to the town council! Just at this assembly, I got his assistant, Tania, to sign it, plus Mrs. Nguyen and Principal Samuels, and . . . well, a bunch of people. Would you guys mind signing, too?"

"Sure!" Paul said, and dashed his name off in ink. He handed the clipboard to Peephole, who flipped through the pages, admiring all the signatures. He signed it and gave it to me, and I signed, too. Dorothea squealed with delight.

"That's five hundred signatures exactly! Now I can submit this to Mayor Pilkington! And if you're really interested in Bellwood's past, you should come over to my house this Saturday at ten a.m. I'm hosting a meeting of the Bellwood Junior Historical Society. I'll have snacks!"

"Bellwood Junior Historical Society?" Paul said. "I didn't know that existed. Are there a lot of members?"

"Yeah!" Dorothea said quickly. "Well, actually, no. This Saturday will be the first meeting. I'll be there, and my little brother, Elvis, and . . . maybe you guys?"

A searing, high-pitched hiss wrenched our attention back to the court. Tania Rose was holding the mic against the big speakers. The crowd quieted instantly.

"Thank you for your attention," she said softly into the mic. "And now Mayor Pilkington would like to say his last few words of the day." With that, she walked back to her seat, her heels clicking in the freshly silent gym.

I got the sense that without her, the mayor wouldn't get much done.

"Um, yes, thank you, Tania. In fact, kids, let's hear it for Tania. She's doing a lot of work on this project, too!"

A few people clapped, and Tania politely waved at the audience, then gestured to the mayor to wrap it up.

"I want to say this to all you young Bellwoodians," Pilkington continued. "You're going to need sunglasses, because your future in Bellwood is bright!"

Principal Samuels stood patiently nearby with her hands clasped behind her back. As soon as the mayor was done, she would hop to the mic to begin the orderly dismissal process. First the green community, seated in the lower rows. Single file, quiet voices. Then the red, in the middle row. Single file, quiet voices. And finally the purple, in the top rows, and that's when the One and Onlys would join the river of students flowing out into the hallways. When she was directing students, she always had the serious expression of an orchestra conductor. I got the sense that she lived for moments like this. I'd heard once that before she became our principal, she'd been an air traffic controller.

"Now here's what I want you to do, Bellwood Middle School," the mayor said, gazing up at the crowd with a broad grin. "I want you to step into the future of Bellwood. Right now. But I don't want you to *walk* into that future. I want you to run! Run like a wild animal into New Bellwood!"

Again, he stepped back and beamed at us. And again, we all glanced at each other, unsure of what to do.

"What are you waiting for? Go! Go! Go!" Pilkington shouted, his fist raised triumphantly. After that, it was too late. Principal Samuels waved and clapped her hands to get our attention, but we couldn't hear her over the roar as we leapt up and stampeded toward the gymnasium doors. Some teachers tried to maintain order by jumping in front of the flood of bodies, but they soon saw that it was no use, and they dodged the rambunctious horde like it was the running of the bulls.

As the students rumbled past, Mayor Pilkington hooted and hollered and handed out rolled-up green bundles. "T-shirts! T-shirts!" he cried. He pointed to Peephole as we walked by. "Hey there, you look like you could use a new T-shirt!"

"Well, I guess I could—"

But Mayor Pilkington was already pulling his right arm back to launch the T-shirt like a football. Instead of putting his hands up to catch it, or jumping to the side, Peephole froze. The T-shirt hit him right in the nose.

"Oof." Peephole clutched his face.

I bent over and picked up the shirt, unfolding it so we could see the design. IT'S A NEW BELLWOOD, it read.

Principal Samuels surveyed the pandemonium and gaped at Mayor Pilkington, looking like she wanted to have him arrested. Tania Rose leaned into the principal, probably offering her words of apology. Meanwhile,

Dorothea Hightower approached Mayor Pilkington with a proud smile, clipboard extended.

"After we go to our lockers, let's meet outside at the bike rack," Paul whisper-shouted above the chaos of the crowd as we followed the procession toward the doors.

I plunged into the scrum of bodies and eventually made it to my locker. After grabbing my backpack, I burst through the back door of the school, where our bikes were locked up.

Paul and Peephole were already there, sniffing the air. I sniffed, too. It was a sweet, sugary kind of aroma. The same smell I'd noticed this morning when I stepped out of the house. We looked around but didn't see anything that could have caused it.

"I don't know about you guys," I said, "but I could go for some ice cream. How about a scoop at Dr. Dave's?"

"I was thinking the same thing," Paul said.

"Choco-Thunder." Peephole nodded. "With sprinkles."

Dr. Dave's was the best, and only, ice cream shop in town. I thought about Mayor Pilkington's New Bellwood speech: it was the only ice cream shop in town—for now, at least.

We were halfway across the schoolyard when we spotted the Beverly brothers under a tall tree. They looked like they were arguing, which was not unusual. Every kid in Bellwood knew that two things were true about Jeb and Zeb Beverly. The first was that they competed in everything. I'd seen them challenge each other over who could do the most push-ups (Jeb won), who could spit the highest into the air without getting hit by the spit when it came down (Zeb won), who could do the best impression of a confused rooster (tie), who could eat the most popcorn-flavored jelly beans without barfing (everybody lost). Even when they decided not to compete, each brother tried to be less competitive than the other.

They'd spotted us, too. "Hey!" Zeb called out. "You guys are like . . . detectives or something, right?"

"That's right," I chimed in, not bothering to conceal my pride that word had gotten around about our sleuthing prowess. "We're the One and Onlys, Bellwood's finest kid detective team."

"Are there other kid detective teams in Bellwood?" Zeb asked.

"Not that we know of," Peephole said. "But if there were, we'd be finer."

"Well, I've got a real mystery for you guys."

"Here we go." Jeb rolled his eyes.

"I *didn't* make it up," Zeb said, sounding oddly serious. "I really did see it. It's up there, I'm telling you."

"See what?" Peephole asked.

"Well . . . ," Zeb started, then sighed and shook his head. "Ah, forget it. You guys wouldn't believe me."

The second thing that everybody knew about Jeb and

Zeb was that they did a lot of things to the truth—bent it, twisted it, ignored it, but rarely ever told it. Well, I'll just say it: they were liars. Jeb once called out "Absent" during roll call in math class even though he was in the first row, because he thought he might get out of the day's quiz. Zeb claimed he couldn't do his science homework because he was allergic to the paper in the textbook.

Still, this sounded promising. Even mysterious. And the One and Onlys were always ready for a new case.

"We've seen a few unbelievable things in our time," I said. "Try us."

Little did I know, we hadn't seen anything yet.

2

At the Top of Funston's Oak

"Jeb bet me I couldn't climb to the top of Funston's Oak," Zeb began. He pointed up at the huge tree towering into the sky. "You know Funston's Oak, right?"

"Of course," I said quickly. It was the tallest tree in the field behind Bellwood Middle School, and every kid in town dreamed of conquering it. But it wasn't just bragging rights that sent generation after generation of Bellwood's youth up into the branchy heights: legend had it that there was a priceless action figure, untouched for decades, on the top limb. The story goes all the way back to the 1950s, when a kid named Benny Funston bet his best friend that he could climb to the top of the tree. His friend wagered his favorite action figure that Benny couldn't. Well, Benny Funston must have been part spider monkey, because he scrambled to the very top. His friend grudgingly forked over the action figure, but the next day, he had regrets. He claimed that because leaves and branches had blocked his view, he hadn't actually *seen* Benny reach the top. He demanded his toy back. Benny immediately climbed up the tree once again and left the figure on the highest limb. His friend was free to get it if he could. His friend tried, but gave up long before the top. And so have countless numbers of young Bellwoodians seeking the action figure. What's so special about it? It's an original Superman action figure from 1939. As in, one of the rarest toys in the world. As in, it's worth tens of thousands of dollars.

"Let me guess," I said. "You chickened out before you reached the top."

Zeb looked offended. "I'll admit that I wanted to turn back a few times, but I just kept thinking about that action figure."

"That's a valuable toy," Paul agreed. "If it's there."

"If it's there," Peephole added, "it's got seven decades of squirrel poop on it. I wouldn't touch it for any amount of money."

"It's not there," Zeb said with certainty.

I blinked at him. "And how do you know?"

"Because I made it to the top of Funston's Oak."

I looked at Paul and Peephole, and their expressions told me they were thinking the same thing: Zeb was full of it.

"It's true," Jeb said in a quiet voice, as if it pained him to admit it. "I saw him up there."

"Don't believe me?" Zeb said. "Fine. But let me tell you this: there's something up there, and it's not Superman."

Paul's curiosity got the better of him. "What is it?"

Zeb leaned in. "A crow," he whispered dramatically.

"That's not unusual, Zeb," I said, disappointed. "Crows live in trees."

Zeb's eyes darted to either side, then he edged even closer. Despite my annoyance, I huddled in closer, too. "This one was a robot."

Paul's eyes grew wide. "A robot?"

Peephole, who distrusted robots, looked nervous.

"It was right above me, poking out of the top of the tree. Its head swiveled all the way around with a weird kind of whirring sound, like a machine. I must have made some kind of noise, because suddenly it looked down at me. Its eyes . . . I'll never forget them . . . they were . . . *red*."

"Prove it," I said.

"How am I supposed to do that?"

"You could climb back up and bring it down with you," Paul suggested.

"No way I'm touching that thing," Zeb said. "For all I know, it'll zap me."

"It won't zap you," I said.

"Oh, you're an expert on robot crows?" Zeb asked.

"No, because they don't exist."

"How about you climb up there and see for yourself?" Zeb said quickly. He nodded, smiling at the idea. "Yeah, then you'll see I'm not making it up. That is, if you think you can make it all the way to the top."

Peephole looked at me uneasily. "That's a pretty dangerous climb, Shanks. I don't think—"

"No sweat," I blurted.

Peephole was right, of course. It was a dangerous climb. If I fell, I'd be splat soup.

Good thing I wasn't afraid of anything.

"You *know* if you get busted climbing the tree, you're in big trouble," Peephole said. He was right about that, too. Principal Samuels had already announced over the intercom (twice) that climbing Funston's Oak was prohibited. In fact, every year, police officers and members of the fire department would come and remind us that nobody should try to climb that tree. My dad constantly told me not to try, but worrying about me was one of his hobbies. Even my mom, who usually encouraged my risk-taking, agreed that it was too dangerous. Basically, every adult in Bellwood wanted to make sure no kid tried to climb Funston's Oak. Of course, all that talk just made me want to try.

We all swiveled our heads to make sure nobody was watching. Getting busted would mean not only that our parents would get involved but also that I wouldn't get the chance to prove to Zeb that he was a liar.

I took off my backpack and did some quick jumping jacks to loosen up. Just as I was about to start the climb, a car on the road caught my attention. Actually, it wasn't a car—it was a lime-green golf cart, driven by Tania Rose, with Mayor Pilkington riding along.

I paused at the bottom of the tree, and Pilkington noticed us and waved. We all waved back. As soon as they turned the corner, I cracked my knuckles in preparation for the climb. "You guys are on lookout duty. If somebody's coming, give me a warning. If I find that action figure, Dr. Dave's on me."

"Mmm," Jeb said. "Strawberry Chunk."

"With sprinkles," Peephole added.

I began climbing. It was easy. My arms and legs were short, but I had a vise-like grip, and I was strong enough to pull myself up onto each branch. Reach, grab, pull, scamper. Reach, grab, pull, scamper. The rule was to not look down. Ever since I was a baby, I loved climbing. My parents always told the story of how I used to climb out of my crib and scale the furniture. I remembered my dad standing still as a statue and letting me claw my way up until I was hugging his head like a koala bear. Reach, grab, pull, scamper. Now my legs started to tremble a little, which meant that I was getting tired. I needed a moment's rest. I hooked my right arm around the trunk and gripped a branch above me.

I broke my rule and looked down to see how far I'd climbed. The ground seemed a lot farther away than I'd expected it to. The Beverly twins were lying belly-down, having an arm-wrestling contest. Peephole had turned his back to the tree, probably because he couldn't bear to watch. Paul was the only one looking up. He gave me a little wave and then a thumbs-up. Out of reflex, I started to return the thumbs-up, but lost my balance for a moment and grabbed the limb. My stomach sank, and my face suddenly felt very hot. I swallowed and tried to slow my breath. This was a weird feeling. I'd climbed plenty of trees before, so why was this time any different? Maybe it was the chicken casserole from lunch coming back to haunt me. *Or maybe,* a voice in my head said, *it's because Funston's Oak is a lot taller than any tree you've ever climbed. If you lose your footing now . . .* I turned the volume down on that voice and kept climbing. Reach, grab, pull, scamper.

Branch by branch, limb by limb, I climbed higher. I convinced myself to focus only on my next move, and eventually I wasn't thinking about the ground—specifically, how far away it was—at all. Before I knew it, I was nearly at the top. I caught my breath and cast my gaze all around me in search of an action figure. Or, I chuckled to myself, *a robot crow.*

And then I heard the noise. A whirring, just like Zeb had described. I looked up, and there it was. Above me, just out of reach. A black bird. Black feathers, spindly black feet. Red eyes.

I couldn't believe it. Zeb's robot crow. Or was it?

"Caw!" I spat, trying to startle it into flight. But it didn't fly away. It didn't even flinch. Suddenly, I remembered the crow I'd seen that morning in my yard. Could it have been the same one?

I reached up, straining on my tippy-toes. My fingers stretched out. If I could just get hold of it, I could bring it down with me. Closer . . . closer . . . almost there . . .

Whirrrrr.

The red eyes locked on me. And then, with a quiet but insistent hum, the crow flapped its wings, quickly shooting up into the air as if propelled by an engine.

Fwip! My sneaker slipped from the branch. Gravity took over, and a weird thing happened as I fell. For a split second, I felt as if I had left my body and was watching myself hurtle downward in slow motion. There I was, my long blond hair floating gently above me like I was underwater. Down, down, down.

It was almost peaceful.

And then—*THWUNK!*

3

Something Is Rotten in the Town of Bellwood

I slammed into a thick limb directly below me. By instinct, my arms clung to it. My feet kicked wildly for a place to stand, and luckily, they found it. A heavy branch.

My legs were shaking, but I had regained my balance. Gravity was defeated again. I breathed. Once. Twice. On the third breath, a little whimper escaped my lips. I was glad nobody was near enough to hear it.

"Everything okay up there?" Paul called. "Did you find the crow?"

My head was swimming, but the breathing helped a little.

"No!" I called out, my voice more of a squawk than I wanted it to be. "I mean, yes. Everything's fine. But—"

Peephole appeared in a frazzle at Paul's side, trying-not-to-shout-shouting up at me, with his hands cupped around his mouth. "Shhhh! Somebody's coming!"

Zeb and Jeb bolted out of sight. Paul and Peephole didn't move a muscle. They knew the golden rule of a good detective team: stick together, even when the ship is going down.

I took a deep breath and let it out, muttering to myself to calm down. My side hurt from the impact, and it would probably be sore for a few days, but I didn't think anything was broken. Lucky.

"It's Mrs. Espinoza!" Peephole barked up the tree.

The smart thing to do would have been to stay up there—hide behind a branch to give Paul and Peephole a chance to get rid of her. But the thought of it made my throat feel tight. Slowly, carefully, I climbed back down, one step at a time, doing my best not to look at the ground. *This isn't you,* I berated myself. *You're supposed to be fearless. Remember?*

"Oh, hello there, Mrs. Espinoza! Lovely day, isn't it?" I heard Peephole say below me in an awkward voice. Acting casual was not something that came easy to him. I don't know if Peephole is the world's *worst* liar, but he's definitely in the top five.

"Tell me, Alexander, what are you and Paul up to?" Mrs. Espinoza's voice was loud and direct. She had been so relaxed earlier today, during class, but now she was getting right to the point.

"Oh, just hanging out under this tree," Paul responded, doing his best to sound unsuspicious.

"That's right, just hanging out under the tree," Peephole said in a rush. "It's such a big tree that we just wanted to sit under it, not try to climb it. Just the two of us, Paul and me, hanging out under this tree."

I released my grip on the lowest branch and landed with a thud on the grass next to Peephole. It wasn't my most graceful dismount, but I was thankful to be back on solid ground.

For the moment, at least.

Mrs. Espinoza stared at me with one hand on her hip. Paul and Peephole were standing next to her with shocked expressions.

"Just the three of us," Peephole said, "like I was saying. Shanks, Paul, and me, hanging out under this—"

Mrs. Espinoza shot Peephole a look, silencing him. Then she narrowed her eyes at me. Her black hair had streaks of brown and was tied up in a loose bun, with strands popping out in all directions.

"Shanks," she said, and my name sounded like an accusation. "Don't you know that climbing this tree is strictly forbidden?"

"I told her it was a bad idea," Peephole said.

So much for sticking together when the ship goes down. If he'd been any closer, I would have kicked him.

"I wasn't really climbing it, though." My mind

scratched around for a reasonable explanation. "I was just . . . um . . . getting a head start on my social studies project."

She raised an eyebrow. "Up there?"

I nodded. "See, I had an idea. Instead of doing my project on one of Bellwood's buildings, I thought I'd focus on the history of our trees. Sort of a *natural* history project. What do you think?"

Mrs. Espinoza squinted at me, tilting her head back and forth. "An interesting idea. But you can study a tree from the ground just as easily as you can from its branches."

"You're absolutely right," I said breezily. "I've learned my lesson about climbing trees."

"Have you?" Her eyes suddenly felt like two heavy weights on me. "Because now you're on my radar. Understood?"

We nodded.

"I hope so. Now, if you'll excuse me, I'm going to get myself some ice cream." With that, she turned and waded slowly back across the field.

"That could've gone a lot worse," Paul said as soon as she was out of earshot.

"Like we could be sitting in the principal's office right now." Peephole exhaled. "And you know how I feel about the principal's office."

You guessed it: Peephole was afraid of it.

"We've got more important things to discuss," I said excitedly. "I can't believe I'm about to say this, but . . . Zeb was telling the truth."

Peephole gawked up at Funston's Oak. "You mean there's a robot up there?"

"Was." I nodded. "I tried to snatch it, but it flew away. But it was a robot, all right. Red eyes, mechanical sounds, the works."

"Whoa," Paul said, his eyes wide in disbelief. His face gradually melted into a grin. "You know what this means?"

"The robot apocalypse is finally here," Peephole said grimly.

"It means the One and Onlys have another mystery to solve," I said, and slapped him on the back. I immediately felt a sharp pain in my side. I winced.

Peephole noticed. "You okay?"

"Me?" I said, then forced a chuckle. "Just stumbled a little up there and banged my side. I'm fine."

"You sure?" I guess my poker face wasn't as good as I thought. My side hurt, but it was more than that. I was rattled, and I didn't want anybody to know. Shanks didn't get scared. I was fearless. It was my thing.

"I said I'm fine." I drew a deep breath and smelled the sweet air. "But if we're going to discuss this case, we're going to need some ice cream. Come on." I hopped on my bike and pedaled for the road. "Let's go to Dr. Dave's and figure out just what a robot crow is doing in Bellwood."

We set off on our bikes across town. At the end of the block, we passed by Waxing Wayne's Carwash-o-Rama, the Daily Buzz Coffee Shop, and the old Brewster House. It was old, all right, with some construction equipment scattered around it. I remembered what Dorothea had said about it being an important part of Bellwood's history—and her own. How? I wondered.

"Maybe you made a mistake," Peephole said. "Maybe it was just a regular crow."

"I thought it *was* a real crow," I called back, "until I got close enough to see its eyes."

"Maybe that's the point," Paul said.

"What do you mean?"

"Think about it," Paul said. "There are crows all over Bellwood, but how often do you notice them? Somebody must have made this thing so that it would blend in and wouldn't attract any attention."

We zipped by good old Honest Hardware, Paul's parents' little store. Mrs. Marconi popped her head out of the bratwurst truck in the parking lot just as we zoomed by.

"Heading to Dr. Dave's!" Paul shouted, and she gave us a thumbs-up.

We cut south on Water Avenue, which took us past the weird porcelain bunny collection adorning Mr. Sherman's front lawn, the trampoline I'd fallen off three times in Mike Hu's yard, and the tiny free library at Mrs. Sandersfeld's house. If we'd kept going, we would've passed by the rec center, where the Lyrical Warriors meetings were held, and then Town Hall, where Mayor Pilkington's office was. But we hung a right onto Pine, where a man in a hard hat and a neon-orange vest was replacing an old fire hydrant, no doubt part of the mayor's town-wide revitalization project. City workers were on every street corner these days, jackhammering and tinkering and repaving and rewiring, determined to make old Bellwood look new and shiny. As we passed, the man turned to me and flashed a smile so bright it seemed to glint in the sun.

"I just know I'm going to have nightmares about robot crows now," Peephole called over his shoulder to us.

"You once had a nightmare about a stick of string cheese that played saxophone," I said. But I had to admit, to myself at least, that there was something creepy about the crow. When its red eyes shifted down to me, it was like it really saw me. And it wasn't a good feeling.

"So," Peephole called, "you're saying that somebody made the crow so it could fly all over town and nobody would notice? Why would they do that?"

"That's what we need to figure out," Paul said.

We'd made it. Dr. Dave's was just up ahead. But something else caught our attention.

"Is that a . . ."

"Giant milkshake?" I said, finishing Paul's question.

Across the street from Dr. Dave's Ice Cream Parlor, a brand-new restaurant had appeared, and yes, there was an enormous milkshake twirling slowly on top of the building like a sleepy ballerina. It was big enough for the Statue of Liberty to take a sip, with a big red-and-white-striped straw poking up from a light red cup decorated with random squiggles and shapes. There was even a splurch of creamy, foamy milkshake dripping down the side of the straw. I knew it was probably made of plaster or something, but my mouth watered anyway as I watched it spin. There was something almost hypnotic about it.

"'Butter Baby's House of Shakes,'" Paul read from the sign on the restaurant.

"Must be one of the new restaurants Pilkington was talking about," I said.

"New Bellwood," Paul muttered.

"It opened up a week or so ago," Peephole said. "I've passed it a few times on my bike, but I haven't tried it yet. There never seems to be anybody there, except the mayor, I guess. His green golf cart is always parked out front."

"That's kind of sad," I said. "They went to all the trouble to build that big milkshake, and nobody is coming in?"

All around us, the air smelled thick and sweet, and my stomach grumbled.

A NOW OPEN neon sign buzzed insistently in the new place's window, and the bright silver-and-red building seemed to glow. I had to admit, there was something about it that drew me in. It was like the place was from a bygone era—the 1950s or '60s—and, at the same time, from the future. My curiosity grew. But across the street, a huge line of customers snaked out the front doors of Dr. Dave's. Bellwoodians were loyal, but their heads still craned curiously in the direction of the mammoth spinning milkshake.

And for a moment, the three of us also paused in the middle of the road, unsure of which place to pedal toward. Dr. Dave's, our old favorite? Or the new, shiny Butter Baby's?

"Choco-Thunder, dudes," Peephole said at last, and we rolled toward the line at Dr. Dave's.

But just as we reached the end of the line, we were blasted with a horrible stench.

"Blech," Peephole spat. "What is that?"

"Smells like a bathroom," Paul said.

All through the line, people reached up to hold their noses.

"Smells like a porta-potty died," I said. "Where's it coming from?"

We swiveled our heads around but saw nothing. The front doors of Dr. Dave's swung open, and Dr. Dave himself stumbled out.

"I'm sorry, folks," he said, pinching his own nose with two fingers. "There must be some kind of sewer leak. A burst pipe, maybe. Construction crews for the New Bellwood project have been making a lot of noise all day, and now they must have knocked something loose."

From the corner of my eye, something caught my attention. Something black and fluttery just above us. A crow? Just as I looked up, a high-pitched screech rang out from the line.

"Rat!"

Peephole's face immediately drained of all color.

"More like rats," Paul observed level-headedly as a scuttling horde of black critters spread out along the crowded line.

"But . . . but," Dr. Dave sputtered, staring in disbelief at the rodents. "I keep my restaurant clean as a whistle! I don't have rats!"

"Looks like you do," somebody called back, "and remind me never to borrow a whistle from you!"

"It's the sewer work," Dr. Dave pleaded. "It has to be. My restaurant is spotless!"

"Let's get out of here!" another voice hollered, and I agreed wholeheartedly.

In one big mob, we all ran across the street to the parking lot of Butter Baby's House of Shakes. The place was bright and clean and free of rats, and the air around it smelled sweet. In the shadow of the massive twirling milkshake, the automatic doors slid open, welcoming us inside like old friends.

4

Poetry from the Top Rope

Mayor Frank Pilkington, dressed in a skintight neon-green leotard with matching arm and knee pads, balanced uneasily on the top rope of the wrestling ring. He pointed down at Mrs. Espinoza, our social studies teacher, who stood in the middle, wearing a black bodysuit with a skull and crossbones on the back.

"Roses are red—" Mayor Pilkington began, then wobbled wildly on the rope, his arms flailing like a windmill. He regained his balance and continued: "Violets are blue, you've got an atomic elbow coming at you!"

Mayor Pilkington attempted to leap off the rope, but lost his footing and crashed down onto the springy mat. Mrs. Espinoza pounced, slapping a headlock on him.

"More cheese puffs, anyone?" Paul asked, tilting the bag to Peephole and me. We were sitting in the safety of the ringside seats. Peephole shook his head distractedly, pouring all his effort into keeping his three-month-old baby sister, Trillium, entertained. He was officially in charge of her when his parents were attending the Monday night Lyrical Warriors meeting. He rolled his eyes and waggled his tongue.

"Please and thank you," I said, plunging my hand in for another fistful of cheese puffs before turning back to the action in the ring.

The meetings had begun a few weeks back, when the Amateur Wrestling Club and the Aspiring Poets Club each booked the Bellwood Recreation Center for the same time. When the two groups showed up and discovered the mistake, they found that a surprising number of amateur wrestlers also had dreams of becoming poets, and vice versa. So, instead of rescheduling one of the meetings, they decided to combine the clubs. Somebody came up with the name the Lyrical Warriors, and everybody loved it. That was that.

"This is a poem titled 'Stomping on Your Foot on a Snowy Evening,'" Mrs. Espinoza barked, struggling to keep the mayor subdued. "Whose ear this is I think I know, his nose is in my armpit, though!"

A chorus of finger snaps came from the ringside spectators. This was the usual reaction to a particularly good line of verse. I licked the cheese dust from my fingers and snapped along.

Up in the ring, Mrs. Espinoza's arms were entangled with Mayor Pilkington's legs. It was impossible to tell who was putting the hold on whom. They agreed it was a stalemate, and rolled free to help each other up.

"Great couplet back there," Mrs. Espinoza said.

"Thanks." The mayor accepted a towel from his ever-present assistant, Tania, and wiped the sweat from his forehead. "That was one terrific chokeslam you had, too."

"Open ring!" a voice declared, and all the members of the club climbed onto the mat together to practice their moves while reciting their best lines of poetry. This was my favorite part.

My parents rolled into the ring and gave me a little wave. I waved a cheese puff back. Their poetry was a little shaky, their wrestling was downright awful, but their costumes were flawless. My mom's wrestling name was Virginia Werewoolf—inspired by her favorite writer, Virginia Woolf—and she wore a long white dress with fake fur around the neck, fangs in her mouth, and a thick black wig. Most people didn't get it, and just thought she was a dog. Under the wig, her hair was short and light brown, nothing at all like mine, but people always said we had the same eyes: bold, fearless, with a hint of mischief.

My dad had the same hair as me, long and blond, but he usually wore his in a ponytail. His wrestling outfit was based on the Specter, his favorite old-timey wrestler. He'd spent hours at home making sure his costume was identical to the original, with every detail perfect, down to the last stitch. A thin gray strip of a mask covered my dad's eyes and was tied at the back of his head. Ash-gray tights hugged his skinny legs, and the long, flowing gray cape that was draped over his shoulders kept getting caught under his feet every fifteen seconds or so. He was working hard on figuring out the Specter's signature move, the Phantom Fling, involving an athletic series of side steps and swoops that dizzied the opponent until a final duck-grab-and-leg-lift relieved them of their balance for good. Judging from the way he kept getting tangled up in the ropes, my dad hadn't perfected it just yet.

My folks were so different from each other. My dad rarely wore shoes and was always finding odd new hobbies to be passionate about. Recently, it had been professional wrestling and making his own tofu. Surprisingly, the homemade tofu was the more dangerous pursuit, as he'd already slipped and fallen—twice—on stray globs. Still, those were better hobbies than his I'm-going-to-teach-myself-how-to-play-trumpet phase, which luckily seemed to be coming to an end.

My mom was a lawyer who moved at about the speed of light and had an entire closet devoted to shoes that she wore only to work. But my parents did have one thing in common: they both loved books. In fact, they'd met in a literature course in college and ended up working on a project together about this creepy old story by a writer named Edgar Allan Poe. The story is about a guy who takes revenge on another guy by burying him alive.

My folks fell in love while working on the project. Isn't that romantic?

Mrs. and Mr. Marconi, Paul's parents, were up in the ring, too, in their Bratwurst Bruiser getups. They both looked like giant sausages, but you could still tell them apart, because Mr. Marconi had mustard on his costume and Mrs. Marconi didn't.

Peephole's parents, Mr. and Mrs. Calloway, were standing awkwardly in the corner of the ring. They were just like their son, only middle-aged. They came for the poetry, and were still not quite on board with the wrestling part. Whenever it was their turn to practice their moves, they were shy and apologetic and kept asking permission before raking people's faces. Right now, Mr. Calloway was taking body-slam pointers from a very hairy-chested masked man in blue tights. The masked man kept insisting that Mr. Calloway should slam him onto the mat, and Mr. Calloway just kept murmuring his no-thank-yous.

"Yuck," Peephole groaned.

I followed his disgusted gaze across the room to where Mrs. Newsome and Mrs. Espinoza were giving each other sips from their Butter Baby's milkshakes and nodding appreciatively.

"The human mouth has over seven hundred species of bacteria in it at any given time," Peephole said. "Sharing straws should be illegal."

"That's a little extreme," I said.

"You don't even want to know how much bacteria is on your toothbrush," Peephole continued. "But go ahead and guess anyway."

"Bad news," Paul said, pointing to Peephole's shoulder. "Trillium spat up on you again."

She certainly had. Peephole's shoulder was drizzled in milky baby barf.

"That's like the fifth time tonight!" Peephole squealed.

"For someone so small and cute, Trillium sure makes a big mess." Paul chuckled.

Peephole didn't think it was too funny. He didn't like messes.

"Hey, look at this," I said, examining the collage of stains on his shoulder. "This one kind of looks like an elephant."

"Oh, yeah, and this one looks like an airplane," Paul agreed.

"Peephole!" I shouted. "Trillium's a baby artistic genius! Don't wipe that up—it could be worth something!"

There were few greater pleasures in life than annoying Peephole.

Grinning to myself, I sat back and surveyed the room. Up in the ring, a cluster of wrestler-poets were stomping their feet and reciting lines, while the rest of the group milled around the seats and the vending machine in the corner. Mrs. Newsome, the poetry teacher from

Bellwood High School, sat sipping her milkshake and coaching Darrel Sullivan on the finer points of rhyming couplets. She'd been sidelined with a broken leg after an aerial assault gone wrong. Darrel sucked at the straw in his own cup, frowning and stroking his bleached white goatee. He glanced over and met my gaze, and his face turned sour, like someone had just shoved a lime in his mouth. I didn't blame him. I'd had sort of a run-in with him last summer while investigating the Case of the Mysterious Rubber Duckies. Things had gotten a little messy between us. Let's just say, Darrel Sullivan wasn't exactly president of the One and Onlys fan club.

In the corner, Mr. Nemo, the local fix-it guy, was taking a screwdriver to the sides of the vending machine between sips of his milkshake. In fact, as I glanced around the room, there were quite a few red milkshake cups from Butter Baby's. I guess everybody else had the same idea we did.

In the opposite corner, Dr. Dave—who did not have a Butter Baby's milkshake in his hand—was talking to Mayor Pilkington. Actually, it looked more like he was talking *at* Mayor Pilkington. Dr. Dave's hands were flying back and forth with emphatic gestures, and he kept leaning in closer to the mayor, who kept leaning farther away. The longer I watched them, the more it seemed that Dr. Dave was angry at the mayor.

"What do you think they're arguing about?" I asked, nodding toward the pair in the corner.

Paul and Peephole followed my nod. "Not sure," Paul said, "but I bet it's got something to do with that sewer leak that was stinking up Dr. Dave's Ice Cream Parlor."

"And the rats," Peephole said, shuddering.

"He was pretty annoyed at all the noise, and he *did* blame the rats and the smell on Pilkington's New Bellwood construction," I said.

"He's probably right," Paul said. "There's work crews all over town. All I ever hear out the window is jackhammers and cement trucks."

"We need some help." We all turned around at the sound of a familiar voice behind us. Jeb and Zeb Beverly were standing there, each holding a can of a different flavor of pop in their hands. "We need somebody to judge our belch-singing contest."

Peephole scooted a few inches away.

"Well, if it isn't the ghosts of Bellwood," I said, fixing them with a sneer. "You sure pulled a quick disappearing act back at Funston's Oak. Ran away at the first sight of Mrs. Espinoza."

"Oh, that?" Zeb said innocently. "We didn't run away . . . we just, uh, remembered that we had a, uh, dentist appointment."

"No cavities." Jeb smiled.

"I bet," I said.

"Well," Zeb began, "did you see the robot crow up there, or what?"

I stared at him hard for a second, then nodded. "Maybe."

"Told you!" Zeb punched his brother on the arm.

"Fine, so there's a robot crow, big deal," Jeb said, rubbing his arm. "Let's get to the contest. It'll be easy. We chug our pop as fast as we can, then the first person to belch-sing 'Twinkle, Twinkle, Little Star'—"

"The *whole* song," Zeb clarified.

"Yeah, that person is the winner."

"But you're also judging who sang it better," Zeb said. "Pitch, emotion, that kind of thing. Ready?"

"Let's get this over with," I said. "On your mark . . . get set . . . chug!"

The twins put the cans to their lips and threw back their heads. Jeb chose grape, Zeb went with orange.

Jeb was the first to finish, tossing his can behind his head and gathering himself for the first note of the song. His mouth moved all around, like he was chewing on a heaping spoonful of invisible peanut butter. Finally, he opened his mouth to belch-belt it out.

"Twiiiiiiink—" he sang, in a surprisingly clear burp-tenor, before a sudden splash of grape foam came flying out of his mouth and onto the floor.

"Hey," I said, "it looks like a gorilla! Look out, Trillium, you've got competition."

Zeb let out a great burp of agreement. "Too bad you didn't get to hear me belch-sing. I've been practicing."

"A shame," Peephole said.

"I guess I should go find a towel and clean that up," Jeb sighed.

"Not if I find one first," Zeb said. They both darted off in hot competition.

I glanced over to the corner again and saw Dr. Dave walking away in a huff from Mayor Pilkington, whose face looked like he'd just been splashed with ice-cold water. Tania Rose patted him on the back in support. I felt bad for the mayor; nobody deserved to be yelled at while wearing neon-green wrestling tights.

Mayor Pilkington and Tania shuffled toward the ring. As they passed by, Darrel Sullivan suddenly appeared and blocked their way. He muttered something that I couldn't hear, and the mayor shook his head distractedly. Tania stepped in front of Darrel and gently led him away.

I strained to overhear their conversation.

". . . all I'm saying is, it seems like an awfully dangerous beverage to have spinning around above the innocent citizens of Bellwood," Darrel said.

"Mr. Sullivan, there is no way the giant milkshake above Butter Baby's is going to topple and fall on your head," Tania said patiently. "I oversaw the construction myself. It's entirely safe."

"Okay, okay." Darrel put his hands up. "But what if somebody accidentally fell into the giant cup and drowned? Have you ever tried to swim through milkshake?"

"It's not actually filled with milkshake, Mr. Sullivan,"

Tania explained, and I detected a hint of annoyance in her voice. "In fact, there's nothing inside there at all except a floor to stand on. And don't worry, the milkshake has a lid—with a trapdoor that you'd have to open in order to fall through. And what would you be doing on top of the milkshake, anyway?"

"Me? I'm not saying *I'd* be up there, but you know, kids do the wildest things. But if somebody *did* fall in and get hurt, that could be a lawsuit, don't you think? Like . . . the town of Bellwood would have to pay somebody a lot if they got hurt by the big Butter Baby's, don't you think?"

I guess Paul wasn't the only person who wasn't so sure about the New Bellwood project.

"Geez," I said to Paul and Peephole, "Darrel Sullivan will do anything to make a quick dollar."

"Actually, I'm kind of scared of the milkshake myself," Peephole admitted. "A milkshake that big? It's just not natural."

A husky yelp from the ring startled the three of us, and we turned just in time to see a great orange blur sailing toward us.

"Look out below!" the blur shrieked.

Peephole stood and spun out of the way in one motion, tucking Trillium's little body to his chest. I'd never seen Peephole move like that. As I was momentarily stunned by this display of cat-like agility from my normally clumsy friend, Paul leapt to safety, too, leaving me in the orange blur's landing spot, with no time to escape.

Crash! Oof! Owf! Urgh!

The orange blur and I rolled around on the floor for a few seconds, trying to get out from under each other.

"Good gracious!" a panicked voice gurgled from the blur. "Are you all right?"

It was Mr. Patel. I should have recognized the orange sweatsuit that he wore to every Lyrical Warriors meeting.

"I'm okay," I said, surprised to find that it was true. Somehow, I'd come out of this disaster without a scratch. But of course, I was the tough One and Only. "You?"

"Fine." Mr. Patel waved the question off, then peered at me for a long second. "Size three. You got a pair of red high-tops this summer. Your dad bought a pair of woven leather sandals, and your mom got a pair of clogs." He and Mrs. Patel owned Bless Shoes, the little store that had been supplying footwear to Bellwoodians for as long as I'd been alive.

"That's right," I said. "You can call me Shanks." We were still on our backs on the floor among the disrupted chairs, but I reached my hand out to shake anyway.

Mr. Patel took it. "Arjun."

Mrs. Patel appeared above us with a look of concern. When she saw that we were both all right, her expression shifted to annoyance. "In the long and proud history of this building, that was the least graceful thing anybody has ever done." She extended a hand to help me up.

"It's okay," I said, "that's what wrestling is all about." I reached down to Mr. Patel, who shook his head quickly and rose to his feet with a groan. And then I turned to Mrs. Patel. "This building has a long history, huh?" I remembered my social studies project for Mrs. Espinoza. Maybe the rec center would be a good subject.

"That's right." She nodded. "But if Arjun's not careful, he'll cause it to collapse."

"Lots of history in this place," Mr. Patel agreed, smoothing out his jumpsuit. "In fact, I saw some of the best wrestling of all time right here in this ring."

Confused, I cast a glance up into the ring, where Mr. Marconi had just attempted a diving moonsault leg drop but ended up on his back. He flopped around in his bratwurst costume, but couldn't manage to turn himself over.

"I'm talking about the Specter," Mr. Patel said, following my eyes. "He could have been the greatest ever. . . ."

"The Specter?" I said. "Like my dad."

Mr. Patel nodded. "But the real thing. He came to Bellwood once, did you know that? It was a long time ago, back in 1962. I was seven years old. A world tour of professional wrestlers was making a stop in little old Bellwood, and my dad brought me here to see them in action. Right up in this ring, I saw the Specter in his last match ever."

"Last match?" Paul asked. I hadn't even noticed that he and Peephole were standing next to us, listening.

"That's right. He was a young star, just about to break into megastardom. But that night, right as he was readying to pin his opponent, something seemed to come over him. He slid out of the ring, disappeared into the crowd, and was never seen again."

"Disappeared?" I echoed. "Why?"

"A mystery," Mr. Patel said, then gave a little salute before bounding back into the ring.

I'd heard of the Specter because he was my dad's favorite wrestler, but I didn't know about his mysterious disappearance. And right here in Bellwood? Not only had I just chosen my building for Mrs. Espinoza's social studies project, but I was beginning to think that Bellwood had a few more secrets than I imagined.

"Another mystery?" Peephole said. "Between the Specter and our robot crow, looks like the One and Onlys have our hands full."

"All this mysteriousness makes me hungry," I said, starting over to the vending machine. Paul and Peephole followed.

Mr. Nemo was just finishing up his repairs as we approached. His long ponytail was black as midnight, but his silver eyebrows and mustache revealed that perhaps his mane would also have been silver without the help of hair dye.

"That thing have any Bozo bars?" I asked. Usually, some chocolaty, peanutty, caramelly gooeyness helped me think.

Mr. Nemo thumbed a sticker reading NEMO to the bottom corner of the machine, then slowly turned to us, his eyebrows arched over his narrow eyes. "You shouldn't sneak up on an old man like that," he said in his usual whispery voice.

I'd never actually had a conversation with Mr. Nemo, but every Bellwoodian knew him from his commercials on local TV, where he'd whisper to the camera, "If Nemo can't fix it, nobody can." He looked the same as he did on TV—narrow, hawk-like face with a silver mustache—but maybe a little older.

"And yes, there are plenty of Bozo bars here for you." He stood up with a few creaks and pops. "Only place in town you can find them."

"What's with the sticker?" I asked, stepping in front of the machine to survey its offerings.

Mr. Nemo glanced down at the machine. "A calling card," he said in a raspy voice. "I leave a sticker on everything I make or fix. I've been in this town so long, there are stickers on just about everything with an ON switch. It's as close to being famous as I ever want to come."

"We're sort of famous, too," I said. "Maybe you've heard of us? The One and Onlys detective team?"

Mr. Nemo stared at us. He blinked.

I thought of our escapades this past summer, when a horde of rubber duckies suddenly appeared on Mr. Babbage's lawn. The three of us chased clues and suspects all over Bellwood until we eventually solved the case at the most epic Triple B in town history. After that, the One and Onlys were famous in our little corner of the world. Okay, maybe not famous. But at least people had heard of us. Some people.

"Detectives, huh?" Mr. Nemo finally said. "But are there any mysteries in Bellwood?"

"You'd be surprised," Paul said.

That was the thing about Bellwood: our little bell-shaped town, surrounded by woods, seemed like your average snoozy hamlet, but if you knew it like the One and Onlys did, you'd know it was filled with all kinds of strangeness. That's why we'd formed the One and Onlys detective team to begin with. Because we suspected there were mysteries lurking among us Bellwoodians. Admittedly, we'd only ever had one real case. But we were always on the lookout for a new mystery to solve.

"Oh, yeah? Then surprise me."

The three of us looked at each other. Should we reveal the details about a case in progress? I couldn't resist the challenge. "Well, you might be surprised to know that there's a robot crow flying around Bellwood as we speak."

"Is that so?" Mr. Nemo perked his eyebrows up again. "Doing what?"

A pause.

"We haven't figured that part out yet," Peephole said. "But we will."

"Soon," I added.

Mr. Nemo nodded, then snapped his toolbox closed. When he turned to us, he was holding out a card. I took it. It read IF NEMO CAN'T FIX IT, NOBODY CAN, along with his contact information.

"If anything breaks during your investigation, give me a call." He slouched down the aisle between the chairs around the ring, turning back to us with a quick wave. "Enjoy that Bozo bar."

And I did.

⇒ 5 ⇐

The Legend of the Specter

"Here's where the Specter is at his most dangerous," my dad said, leaning closer to the TV. "See, Shanks?"

"I see," I said through a mouthful of bagel and cream cheese—my preferred bedtime snack. The TV flickered with black-and-white images of a gigantic wrestler, Gorilla Monsoon, circling an ant of a man in a mask and cape.

"Now, Gorilla Monsoon thinks he's going to gobble this guy up, but the Specter's too quick. Here it comes . . . here it COMES. . . ." My dad leapt to his feet. "The Specter's got him all twisted around, and now . . . yes!! *Whoosh!*" He swung his bagel in front of him. "The Phantom Fling!" My dad darted around in front of the TV, trying to mimic the graceful lunges of the Specter, but he looked more like a squirrel in a hailstorm. "Down goes Gorilla! Down goes Gorilla!" He laughed and collapsed back onto the couch next to me, slapping my knee.

When we came home from the Lyrical Warriors meeting earlier that night, I was thinking about what Mr. Patel had said about the rec center's history—and especially about the mysterious disappearance of the wrestler known as the Specter. I asked my dad about it, and the words had barely made it past my lips when he lunged to his feet in excitement. Like an eager dog fetching his own leash, he ran to his room to grab his old Specter wrestling tapes, and he sat me down on the couch to teach me all about his favorite wrestler.

The Specter was tiny in stature, but he bounced and twirled around the ring as quick as lightning. My dad was about the same height and build, and he tried to emulate his style in the ring. Unfortunately, he didn't share any of the Specter's skills. Still, he had the enthusiasm, and that counted for something.

I took another big bite of my bagel and watched as the ringside reporter tried to corral the Specter into a post-match interview. But just as the reporter uttered a question into the microphone, the Specter seemed to melt away from view, twirling quietly back into the boisterous crowd behind him. It was almost . . . ghostly.

"Kayfabe," my dad said, pronouncing the word slowly through a mouthful of his own bagel.

"Huh?"

"*Kayfabe*," he repeated. "It's a word for the way wrestlers never break character. You've got to keep up the illusion, for the sake of the audience." He turned to me. "Now, you know that they're not actually fighting, of course," my dad said, reminding me for the hundredth time that wrestling was fake, which everybody on the planet knows.

"Oh, really? So this shouldn't hurt?" I sprang up and threw my arms around his neck in a headlock.

"You got cream cheese in my hair!" he squawked.

I tightened my grip, and felt a sharp pain in my side. I let out a little yelp.

My dad pulled away from me and frowned. "What's the matter? You hurt yourself?"

"Just stumbled a little climbing a tree earlier," I said. "It's just a bruise, no big deal."

But he reacted in the way I knew he would, with a look of horrified concern. "Climbing a tree? What tree?"

"I don't know." I shrugged. "Just a tree." If I had said Funston's Oak, I'm sure his head would have exploded.

"Was it a big fall? Did you land correctly? Remember to tuck and roll to absorb the impact?"

"Dad, I'm fine!" I said.

"But—"

"If she says she's fine, then she's fine, Wes," my mom chimed in from the kitchen table, where she usually worked until late into the night.

"It's not that I don't trust you, honey," my dad said, "it's just that you're such a . . . daredevil . . . and I *love* that about you, but you know I worry."

My dad had been worried about me from the day I was born, and I knew that's what parents did. And it's not that my mom didn't worry—she definitely did—but she was tough, just like me, and she knew that to keep being tough, I had to grab life by the collar and shake it around a little bit.

"Mom's right. I can handle myself. But I have another question about the Specter," I said, trying to change the subject. "Mr. Patel said that he saw the Specter wrestle live, in person, at the Bellwood Recreation Center, like, a million years ago."

"Arjun was *there?*" my dad said in awe. "Back in '62?"

I nodded. "And he said it was the last time the Specter ever wrestled. Do you know what happened to him? If he was so good, how come he never wrestled again?"

My dad leaned back and laid a meaningful gaze on me. He looked like he was getting ready to tell me the most important thing ever.

"He was better than good," he began. "He could have been the best there ever was, if only he hadn't . . ." My dad shook his head, as if to refocus his thoughts. "The legend of the Specter began in December of 1961, at a small community recreation center in Schuylerville. That was where the Specter made his first appearance."

"Schuylerville?" I said. "That's not far from Bellwood."

"That's right," my dad said. "Only about twenty miles down the road. There, before a small audience, the Specter first showcased his cat-like quickness and amazing tumbling ability against a much larger opponent, Bear Bumley. The Specter was very small, but his smooth, lightning-fast moves made him as hard to catch as a ghost. The audiences loved to see him wrestle much larger opponents and confound them with his speed.

"Night after night, week after week, the Specter danced around the ring, quickly becoming a crowd favorite. Within a few months, he'd started wrestling in larger auditoriums, performing in front of thousands of eager spectators. Before long, fans were chanting his name."

As my dad talked, black-and-white images of the Specter flashed on our TV screen. The Specter balancing on the ropes, facing the audience and holding his finger to his lips in his trademark pose. The Specter suspended mid-leap, his arms and legs outstretched into a flying star. The Specter peering down at his opponent on the mat while the referee held his fist up in triumph. The Specter backing into a mass of fans, already seeming to melt away into the crowd.

"That's when he developed his unique strategy of wearing down his much larger opponents as they chased him around the ring. When they were finally exhausted, he would bring them down to the mat with his signature move—"

"The Phantom Fling!" I said.

"That's right!" My dad leapt to his feet and mimicked the one-two-three maneuver. On the third step, he lost his balance and crashed into the coffee table.

"You okay, Dad?" I extended a hand to help him up.

"Fine, fine," he said, dusting himself off. "Now, where was I? Oh, yeah . . . before long, the Specter hit the big time. Within five months of his debut in Schuylerville, the Specter was wrestling in sold-out arenas in New York City, Los Angeles, and every major metropolis in between. Adoring fans filled the seats, chanting for the Specter, dressed in his classic gray mask and cape, to perform the Phantom Fling. But the more attention and fame the Specter received, the more he seemed to avoid the limelight. He stopped doing post-match interviews, and he never hung around the arenas very long."

I took a bite of my bagel and chewed slowly. It was weird to imagine somebody doing something as attention-grabbing as dressing up in a costume and wrestling another person onstage, then shying away from the fame. But if there was one thing I'd learned as a detective, it was that people were complicated animals.

"Still, the more he avoided attention," my dad continued, "the more popular he became. And then it was announced: in late June 1962, the Specter would get a shot at the championship belt. In a title match in front of a sold-out crowd in Chicago, the Specter would wrestle the feared Killer Kowalski."

"He sounds mean," I said.

"He *was*. Once took a guy's ear off in a match."

"Ouch."

"Yeah, but nobody could stop the Specter. He was shooting like a rocket straight to the top of the wrestling world. But that all changed the night of June 15, 1962. In a tune-up match a week before the title bout, the Specter found himself in a small venue in a tiny town near Schuylerville, where his journey had begun six short months before."

"In Bellwood?" I asked.

My dad nodded. "He was supposed to wrestle a no-name opponent, please the fans that had paid money to see him and his signature Phantom Fling, then rest a few days before the title match in Chicago. Everything was going according to plan," my dad continued. "The Specter had worked his opponent into an exhausted stupor. The crowd chanted 'Phantom Fling! Phantom Fling!' The Specter seemed poised to perform his famous move and pin his opponent. But that's not what he did. . . ."

"What happened?" my mom asked from the kitchen table. She'd put down her work and was listening intently.

My dad shrugged. "He left."

"He *left*?" I repeated. "What do you mean?"

"I mean he left. He slid out of the ring instead of pinning his opponent. He vanished into the confused crowd."

"And then what?"

"And then . . . nothing. Nobody ever heard from the Specter again."

"But . . . *why*?"

"There are lots of theories. Some people say he was running from somebody. Some people think that he didn't want any part of the fame that was coming his way. Others say his disappearance was the ultimate form of kayfabe. He played the part of the ghost right up until he vanished like one."

"What do you think happened to him?" I asked.

My dad tilted his head in contemplation. "Maybe he wanted to hide. And sometimes, the best place to hide is in plain sight."

"Really?" I said, doubtful. "That strategy doesn't work well in hide-and-seek." But then I thought of the robot crow and what Paul had said about it blending in. Maybe there was something to this idea of hiding in plain sight.

"Well, the whole thing is a mystery. And I think it would take a good detective to solve it. Know any?" He winked at me.

I grinned. My dad was right: it was a good mystery, and I couldn't help wondering why the Specter had slipped out of the ring that night in Bellwood all those years ago. Maybe, if I did my social studies project on the Bellwood Recreation Center, I could get to the bottom of the mystery of the Specter.

Something attracted my attention and reminded me that the One and Onlys already had a mystery on our hands. From the kitchen window, I could see a black bird perched on a branch. Its eyes seemed to be staring right at me.

I stood and moved toward the window slowly.

"Shanks?" my dad said. "Everything okay?"

"I think this crow is staring at me . . . ," I whispered, creeping ever closer to the window.

"The crow is . . . staring at you?" my mom asked. "You know what that reminds me of, Wes?"

" 'The Raven'!" My dad snapped his fingers and nodded. "I was thinking the same thing."

"What's that?" I said, edging still closer to the window.

"It's a poem by Edgar Allan Poe about a big black bird that haunts this rich guy after his wife dies. I recited it to your mother on our first date."

"I'm surprised there was a second date," I said. I inched close enough to make eye contact with the bird. Its black eyes blinked twice, then, with a quick flutter, it disappeared from view. There, on the branch where it had been sitting, was a white gloop.

"Never mind," I said. "It pooped."

Both my parents flashed me quizzical looks. "That didn't happen in the poem," my mom said.

I guess they were used to weird behavior from me, because my mom went back to shuffling through her papers on the kitchen table, and my dad picked up his trumpet. A moment later, an unceremonious honk rang out.

I turned back to the empty spot on the branch where the crow had just been. One thing was crystal clear to me. To make any progress in our investigation, the One and Onlys were going to have to get our hands on that robot crow.

Tomorrow after school, we'd begin our search.

6

Chasing Crows

The next day at school oozed by achingly slow. In English, somebody ripped notebook paper out really loud at the beginning of the class, and for the next twenty minutes, Mrs. Nguyen let out volcano breaths to calm herself down. In PE, Teddy Spartacus cheated at broomball, and it took a restorative circle to restore order. In math, Mr. McClelland was discussing the difference between a concave and a convex hexagon when Mitzi Peters raised her hand and asked if there was a different desk she could sit at because hers was for a right-handed person, and when Mr. McClelland said no, she started reciting a list of problems only left-handed people have, and when she got to can openers and slow-drying pens, she screamed because she saw a spider, which prompted Eduardo Blackman to jump up and squash it with his foot, but then everybody laughed when they discovered it wasn't a spider but a Raisinet, but then Mr. McClelland got mad when Eduardo ate it. In the cafeteria, the One and Onlys performed an autopsy on the chicken casserole, which, it seemed, had died a long time before lunch. Finally, at the glorious clanging of the last bell, I joined a gushing river of students spilling into the hallways. After a quick stop at my locker to pick up a black case— a special investigative tool that I'd had to borrow from my dad—I opened the doors and walked out into a sunny Tuesday afternoon.

There was a robot crow on the loose in Bellwood, and it was time for the One and Onlys to track it down.

Paul and Peephole met me under Funston's Oak, just like I'd asked them to. Peephole stared up into the leafy heights and shook his head. "This again? I thought we agreed we weren't climbing this tree anymore."

"We're not," I said. "At least, we *might* not be. Did you bring what I asked?"

Peephole reached into his backpack, pulled out a huge pair of binoculars, and hung them around his neck.

I slid the black case off my shoulder, unzipped it, and lifted the brass instrument out.

"What's that?" Peephole asked.

"Never seen a trumpet before?" I said.

"I've never seen *you* with a trumpet before. Do you know how to play that thing?"

"My dad let me borrow it, and of course I know how

to play it. You blow as hard as you can into this part, and the music comes out of the other part."

"Pretty sure it's a little more complicated than that," Peephole said.

I waved off the conversation. "My trumpet playing doesn't have to be good, it just has to be loud."

"Okay, I'm intrigued," Paul said. "How is this going to help us capture that robot crow?"

I gazed up at Funston's Oak. "What do all crows have in common?"

"They're all trying to poop on my head?" Peephole asked.

"Um, no, and that's kind of paranoid." I held up the trumpet. "They all fly away when they're startled by a loud sound."

"I see." A grin curled Paul's lip. "So we go around Bellwood blowing your horn, startling birds out of trees, and . . ."

"And any crow that doesn't fly away must not be a real crow. It must be—"

"—a robot! Genius!" Paul said.

"Actually, I think it's kind of silly," Peephole said. "And did you know that crows have long memories? They can recognize people's faces, even if they've only seen you once. When I was seven, I accidentally hit a crow with a baseball. Since then, I've been pooped on by crows six times. Still think I'm paranoid?"

"Maybe crows are like dogs," I suggested. "You know,

when you run, they chase. The crows probably sense you're scared of getting pooped on, so they aim right at you. Besides, do you have a better idea?"

Peephole considered this, then shrugged. "Nope. Let's do it."

"Okay, let's start here, then make our way through the center of town, all over the west side, loop around the bottom of Bellwood, then come up the east side," Paul said. "We've got to be thorough. If there's an android bird out there, we'll find it."

I brought the trumpet to my lips and blew up at Funston's Oak as hard as I could. The instrument didn't make a sound.

"Is this thing broken?" I asked.

"I told you it took more than just blowing," Peephole said. "You have to do your lips like this." He puckered them up in a way that looked like he'd just eaten ice cream so cold that it froze his teeth.

I raised the trumpet and tried it again, copying Peephole's face.

Amazingly, this time it worked. In fact, the relative quiet of the field was shattered by the brassy shriek. Instantly, a black flutter rose from the top of the tree, and all the crows escaped into the sky.

"See any stragglers?" Paul asked.

"Nope," Peephole said, peering through his enormous binoculars. "No robot crow here. Let's keep looking."

We hopped on our bikes and set off, rolling steadily

down the street away from the middle school, ogling the treetops. We hung a right onto McGillicuddy, and Paul cried, "There!"

It was a tall tree, an elm, I think, with a gathering of crows near the top. We jumped off our bikes and ran to the trunk, where I let out another tinny squeal of the trumpet.

Every crow fluttered quickly into the air. One or two let out an alarmed *Caw!*

We pushed on down the road. On Buckman Street, we found three trees filled with crows, but none were left behind in any of them after the trumpet's wail. On Kenilworth Road, we frightened all the crows out of a maple, and a snoozing old man out of his hammock. When he got to his feet, he rubbed his eyes, blinked, and declared that he could really go for a milkshake. On Radford, our fellow sixth grader Chad Foster saw us from his window and came out to meet us with his trombone. He gave me some quick pointers on playing the horn, then joined us on our mission all the way down his block. He asked five or six questions about the trumpet itself, but never once inquired as to why we were trying to scare crows from the trees with it. Near the bottom of Bellwood, Mr. Babbage, the Bratwurst King, waved to us from his porch and asked me to play the national anthem. I said okay, then proceeded to blow out a long succession of notes that sounded like a goose had its wing caught in a door. All of the crows escaped the tree in his front yard, while his little dog frantically yipped and yapped. When I was done, Mr. Babbage smiled politely, thanked me, and suggested I keep practicing.

We had scoured the west and south sides of Bellwood and were just coming back up the east side when we stopped to rest on Bronson Avenue.

"My lips are numb," I said, "and we've managed to make an enemy out of just about every crow in Bellwood. Was this a bad idea?"

"I believe I'm already on record about that," Peephole muttered. "I think we should quit before we're the victims of an aerial excrement attack." He lifted his eyes to a short, leafy maple in a front yard across the street. "That one's got a crow," he sighed. "Might as well try it and then call it a day."

I wasn't one for giving up, but I was coming around to Peephole's point of view. Maybe the plan was a teensy bit stupid.

The three of us rolled our bikes over to the tree. I brought the trumpet up to my mouth once more and belted out an awkward honk. Peephole aimed his binoculars skyward. "It's not moving. Play it again, Shanks."

Once again I lifted the trumpet to my lips, and this time I blew with all my might. A piercing note rang out.

"Still not moving," Peephole said. He lowered the binoculars and shuddered. "Do you think . . . ?"

"Only one way to find out," I said, laying the trumpet at my feet and readying for a climb. It wasn't a particularly tall tree—nothing at all like Funston's Oak—and I guessed it would be a pretty easy time going up.

I mapped out my route, jumped to grab a branch, and began pulling myself up. Like I'd guessed, it was a simple climb, and before I knew it, I was getting close to the crow. Sure enough, it wasn't moving. In fact, it reminded me of the crow I'd seen in my yard yesterday. Just . . . perched there, completely still, like it had been turned off. I was about to reach up and take hold of the next branch, but I stole a quick peek down at my feet. And that's when something inside gave way, like a bridge suddenly crumbling. I wrapped one arm around the trunk and hugged it, putting my other hand up to my chest. For the first time in my life, I became aware of my breathing. Every breath, in and out, and all the work it took just to keep breathing. What if I breathed out but couldn't breathe back in? What if my lungs couldn't fill back up with air? I got dizzy. It felt like somebody had poured a bucket of dirty water into my head. I tried to swallow, but my mouth had no moisture at all.

I remembered the feeling of nearly falling from the top of Funston's Oak. Tiny stars started dotting my vision. My face suddenly felt hot. What was happening to me?

With shaking arms and legs, I climbed back down the tree, not even realizing I'd made it back to the ground until I stumbled to my hands and knees.

"What happened?" Paul asked. "Are you okay? You look like you saw a monster up there."

I wanted to tell them what had happened. About the horrible feeling of panic that struck me up in the tree, just like it had in Funston's Oak. Instead, I shook my head and forced out a chuckle.

"It's my side," I lied. "It hurts too much. I'm okay, but I don't think I can climb anymore."

He stared at me for a second too long, then said, "I'm going up."

"You are?" Peephole and I said together. Paul was a heck of a detective, but he wasn't the greatest tree climber.

A high, spastic howl came from the house we were standing in front of. We turned to see a small, mean-looking dog pressed against a window. Judging by its vicious wiggles and barking, it wasn't a fan of us hanging around.

"There's no way I'm letting this mystery go," Paul said, turning back to the tree. With resolve in his eyes, he jumped up, grabbed the bottom branch, and scrambled up the trunk. He was a slow climber, but a steady one, and before long, he was halfway up the tree, nearing the branch where the unmoving crow sat.

"It's okay to be scared, you know," Peephole said quietly, still looking straight up into the tree.

"Ex*cuse* me?" I said.

"You're scared" he said in the same matter-of-fact voice. He turned to me. "I recognize that look in your eye. Trust me. I see it just about every time I look in the mirror."

"I don't get scared," I scoffed.

The angry little dog in the house howled again, scraping its claws against the window.

Peephole kept staring. "What did you see? A rabid fox? A mutated squirrel? Or was it just boring, old-fashioned fear of heights?"

"I'm telling you, I'm *not* scared," I said, annoyed. Was it that obvious? Could Paul tell? Would everybody be able to tell that I was suddenly a scaredy-cat?

"You can admit it to me," Peephole said. "I might even be able to give you a few pointers."

He was right, of course. I was scared, and I shouldn't have denied it. This could have been my chance to talk about it. But I didn't want to talk about it. I didn't want to admit it. A word popped into my head: "kayfabe." Like a professional wrestler, I had to stay in character. I had to be tough Shanks. *You've got to keep up the illusion.*

"Dude, you're out of your mind," I said, shaking my head.

The sound of a car drew our eyes to the road. A red sedan was rolling up Bronson Avenue toward us.

"We don't want to attract attention," I said to Peephole, "so don't look up in the tree. Just act casual."

"Uh-oh," Peephole said. "The car is slowing down."

"It'll pass," I said calmly. "Just act casual."

"Uhh-ohh," Peephole repeated, drawing each syllable out even more, as the car began to turn into the driveway.

The furious little dog in the house suddenly stopped barking, shifting its attention to the car. Its tail began wagging.

"Don't look up at the tree," I repeated under my breath.

The car parked in the driveway, and the driver's door swung open.

"Uhhhh—" Peephole croaked.

Mrs. Espinoza, our social studies teacher, emerged from the car, peering over at us with a curious face.

"Casual, dude," I hissed.

"What's casual?" Peephole whimpered back. "What does a casual person do? Is running away casual? Because Mrs. Espinoza said that if she caught us up in a tree again, then—"

"Paul!" I whisper-shouted, interrupting Peephole's meltdown. "If you can hear me . . . stay . . . in . . . the . . . tree." I turned to Peephole. "Just smile."

This whole thing felt weirdly déjà vu–ish.

I waved at Mrs. Espinoza, who was approaching us across her lawn.

"Shanks? Alexander? What are you up to?"

"Not much," I said breezily. "Just out for a bike ride, getting some exercise. Is this your house?"

Mrs. Espinoza stopped a few feet in front of us,

pushing the mahogany-streaked black hair out of her face. "Sure is," she said, then looked over at Peephole, who was blasting out a million-watt smile. Her gaze lingered a little too long, and it seemed like she was suspicious.

The dog in the house let loose a frantic, high-pitched roar, scraping at the glass again.

Mrs. Espinoza turned to the house. "Meatball!" she called out. "That's no way to behave!" She turned back to us. "He's very sweet, but he thinks everybody is up to no good."

"I don't blame him," I said. "You can never be too careful. Strange things have been known to happen in Bellwood."

"Is that right?" Mrs. Espinoza stole a glance up the tree. "Shanks, are you still planning on doing your project on the trees of Bellwood?" She craned her head up and squinted.

I quickly lifted the trumpet to my lips.

Squeeeenk!

Mrs. Espinoza and Peephole jumped back, startled by the sudden noise. She looked down at me in shock, which was better than her looking up at the tree. From inside the house, Meatball barked his disapproval.

"Sorry." I chuckled innocently. "And no, actually, I decided to do my project on the Bellwood Recreation Center."

"Oh?"

"Yep, lots of good history there," I said. "Did you know it was where the Specter had his last recorded appearance?"

"Interesting," Mrs. Espinoza said. "And how about you, Peephole? What are you doing your project on?"

Peephole was still smiling, but the color drained from his face. I knew that he hadn't chosen a topic, and it was slowly eating him alive. "Working on it," he peeped out.

"Well, you'll probably need to get in there and feed Meatball or something, so—"

"Taking a bike ride with that?" Mrs. Espinoza pointed to the trumpet in my hand.

"Oh, yeah. Well . . ."

"Training," Peephole blurted out. We both turned to look at him. If he'd smiled any wider, he would have eaten his own head. "Training for . . . marching band," he stammered. "Did you hear? They're considering changing it from a marching band to a . . . pedaling band."

"A pedaling band?" Mrs. Espinoza repeated.

I slapped my forehead and screamed—all in my head, of course.

"That's right." Peephole grinned maniacally. "Or not. They aren't sure yet. They may change it to a pedaling band, or they may not. Might or might not do that. Nobody knows."

"And where's your friend?"

"Our friend?" I said, surprised. "It's just me and Peephole here."

"But I see three bikes." She pointed to our discarded bikes on the sidewalk.

Peephole started to respond, but I jumped in ahead. "Oh, yeah, that's Paul's bike. See, he got picked up from school today, and so he asked us to walk his bike home for him."

Mrs. Espinoza stared at me and raised her chin, as if she was trying to read a note in bad handwriting. "Can I ask you a question?"

"Sure, why not?" I said.

"Why do I always get the sense that you are hiding something?"

I had to admit, I didn't expect *that* question. But like I said, Mrs. Espinoza had teacher superpowers, and one of them was asking really uncomfortable questions.

I opened my lips to speak, but nothing came out. Which was too bad, because then Peephole started talking.

"Hiding something? Us? Me? Nope, couldn't be. I don't hide anything. I *can't* hide anything. I am horrible at hiding. You know what game I'm awful at? Hide-and-seek. In fact, even if I *wanted* to hide something, I wouldn't know where—"

"You're right," I said, as sheepishly as I could. "We *are* hiding something." I held up the trumpet. "This is my dad's . . . and I took it without asking permission.

I was worried that you might mention it to him at the next Lyrical Warriors meeting. If he found out I took it, he'd flip out."

Peephole twirled to look at me, his smile changing to a look of shock. "You said he was cool with it."

I shot him a quick laser glare, then said, "Yeah, I guess I lied. So . . . that's why we were acting weird. But, wow, we really must be going, right, Peephole?"

He flashed his smile again and nodded.

"Good chatting with you, Mrs. Espinoza. See you in school!"

We all stood there nodding at each other, but nobody moved an inch. I waited a few seconds, and then it became clear that we were going to have to ride away. And leave Paul stranded up in the tree.

Peephole and I rolled our bikes—and Paul's—out onto the street, waving a polite goodbye to Mrs. Espinoza, who finally turned and walked across her lawn to her front door.

"We abandoned Paul!" Peephole said as we walked away from Mrs. Espinoza's house.

"We had to," I said. "Besides, we didn't abandon him. We're going to loop into Mrs. Espinoza's backyard, find a place to hide, and wait for Paul to come down from the tree."

"But if Mrs. Espinoza sees us—"

"She won't!" I said, busting a right down a driveway that led to a backyard. From there, Peephole followed as

I trundled my way back to Mrs. Espinoza's. We ducked down behind a log at the edge of the woods behind her house. From there, we could just barely see the tree that Paul was hiding in.

For a long minute, our eyes darted between the tree and the house while we waited for Paul to drop or for Mrs. Espinoza to emerge. Finally, a pair of sneakers dangled from the foliage of the tree in the front yard for a second or two, and then the rest of Paul came thumping back to earth. He gathered his balance and stole a quick glance at the house, then bolted toward us, carrying something under his arm like a football.

In a few short seconds, he crossed the backyard and made for the woods, collapsing at our side, panting. His red face was glistening with sweat. I expected to see relief in his eyes. I didn't.

"I have it," he said in a strange whisper.

He held out his arm to show us. There, staring up at us with blank eyes, was a crow. It looked like a regular crow, but it was utterly lifeless.

"Whoa," I said.

With a loud creak, the back door swung open to reveal Mrs. Espinoza.

"Out, Meatball!" we heard her say. "You're just too noisy!"

The furry little demon trotted out of the house and paused in the backyard, glancing over his shoulder when the door thwacked shut.

We crouched down behind the log as Meatball pointed his noise toward the woods.

"Do you think he sees us?" Paul asked.

I shook my head.

Peephole popped his head up like a periscope. Meatball immediately released a tornado of growls and barks.

"Yep, he sees us!" Peephole cried. He sprang to his feet. "And he's coming right at us!"

"Into the woods!" I yelled. "And don't lose that robot crow!"

⇒ 7 ⇐

A Closer Inspection

We bumped across the rough terrain as Meatball careened toward us so fast that his tongue flapped out of his mouth. He was a tiny blur of fur and ears and teeth and rage.

Beyond him, I caught a glimpse of Mrs. Espinoza coming out into the yard to see what the trouble was. I ducked over my handlebars, praying that she wouldn't see us.

"We need to split up!" Paul shouted.

"Meet at headquarters!" Peephole said, and he splintered off to the right.

Paul hooked left, and I kept on straight. It was a good strategy. Meatball could only choose one of us to follow.

He chose me. I pedaled faster and faster, weaving in and out of trees and wrenching my handlebars as I swerved around loose logs and sudden dips, but Meatball's little legs were churning closer and closer to me. The sun was going down, which made it hard to see, and there were about a million things in my way. Luckily, I spotted an opening in the trees ahead of me. Everyone knew the Bell Woods was crisscrossed with old service roads, and maybe this one would give me an open track to get up some real speed. I pointed my front tire at the clearing and chugged away.

Meatball was nipping at my back tire as I blasted out of the trees and into the pale twilight of the old road. The little dog leapt at me with his mouth open, but he sailed past when I cut to the left. Now, with an open stretch ahead of me, I stood up and pedaled as hard as I could. Meatball regained his balance, but within a few seconds, he gave up, and I threw a farewell wave over my shoulder as I zoomed deeper into the woods, headed for the safety of the One and Onlys' secret headquarters.

"Is it looking at me?" Peephole asked. "Crows can carry a grudge, you know." He was sitting a few feet away from us on his own log, giving the crow some space. Next to him was a row of rubber duckies, souvenirs of our last case, and behind him, nailed to a thick tree, was our hand-carved wooden sign reading ONE AND ONLYS. This was actually our second super-secret team headquarters, in the middle of the Bell Woods: the first one had been demolished when the Conquistador megastore was built.

Paul and I sat next to each other on our own tree stumps, the robot crow on the ground at our feet.

"Well, this crow is a robot, so I don't think the same rules apply," Paul said. "Hey, Shanks, didn't you say the crow you saw in the tree had red eyes?"

"It did," I said. This crow's eyes were black, not red. "Must be turned off. Or maybe it ran out of batteries or something."

"It's freaking me out," Peephole declared.

Just about everything freaked Peephole out, but this time, I agreed with him. It was exactly the size, shape, and color of a real crow, but its black eyes had an intense nothingness to them that was . . . well . . . freaky. Its legs, feet, and beak were metal, which made it a little heavy to hold in your hands.

"Maybe some crazy inventor made a bunch of mechanical animals for fun," I suggested, "and just let them loose. Or maybe it *wasn't* for fun. Maybe it's a diabolical plan to take over Bellwood with an army of android critters."

"That's ridiculous," Peephole said—but it sounded like he was trying to convince himself more than me.

"Maybe it's too late." I kept going, because I could see Peephole was getting annoyed. "And maybe it's not just animals. Maybe it's robot people . . . robot . . . BABIES! Peephole! Trill is a robot! Don't turn your back on her! Don't trust—"

"Guys, focus!" Paul said. "We've got a real live mystery here that needs solving."

"Does it talk?" Peephole asked.

"Why don't you ask it?" I suggested.

Peephole leaned forward and, in a loud, slow voice, asked, "Where did you come from?"

I'm not sure who looked sillier, Peephole talking to a robot crow or me and Paul listening for a response.

I poked the thing with a twig. "It looks so real."

"Exactly," Paul said. "Now that we've got our hands on it, we need to figure out who made it and why they wanted to fly it all over Bellwood without anyone noticing. Let's see if there are any clues."

Paul picked up the crow, turned it around carefully, and ran his fingers over its feathers.

"Hey, what's this?" Paul pushed a feather to the side with his thumb. "There's something under here."

He was right. Under the feather, stuck to the hard plastic body of the crow, was a small white sticker with some handwritten scribbling. But the thing we all noticed first was the single word printed in the center of the sticker.

"'Nemo,'" I read.

"Whoa," Paul said, sitting up straight. "Mr. Nemo *did*

say he put a sticker on everything he made. I guess we have an answer to the first question."

"So the guy who fixes toasters and vending machines all over town made this thing?" Peephole said, inching closer. "But . . . why?"

"There's something else written on the sticker," Paul said. It was hard to make out the words. Not only were they scribbled very small, they were also in cursive and a little smudged.

"Does that say . . . 'Perch in Pig Meat Shop'?" Peephole guessed.

"No, that's a *B*, not a *P*," Paul said. "'Perch in Big . . .'"

"'. . . Left Shoe,'" I finished.

"Big left shoe?" Peephole said. "What is that supposed to mean?"

I shook my head. "It says 'perch,' so maybe this thing lives in some kind of big left shoe when it's not flying around town?"

"How could it live in a shoe?" Peephole asked.

"Beats me," I said, taking the crow from Paul. "It must be remote-controlled, right? So maybe Mr. Nemo operates it from—"

A strange noise, like a mechanical clicking, interrupted me. It was coming from the robot crow. As we watched, its black eyes suddenly glowed red, and its little black beak opened slightly.

"What's it doing?" Peephole stepped back.

"I think it's turning on," I said. "Maybe it's—"

I was interrupted again. This time, a hissing emanated from its beak, accompanied by a fine mist. Startled, I dropped the crow to the ground and scampered backward.

"What was that?" I yelped.

Paul bolted from the crow, too, and Peephole was already a good fifteen feet away, behind a tree.

And then it hit us. The smell. Well, the putrid stink of a thousand overflowing sewers would be a better way to describe it.

"What is *that*?" I croaked again.

"That stink," Paul said, covering his nose with his shirt, "the crow sprayed it out!"

And then, while we struggled to hold our breath, the bird suddenly lifted into the air with an insistent hum.

"It's getting away!" I yelled, and just as I did, the bird twirled to swoop directly at me.

"Look out, Shanks!" Paul yelled.

I did the only thing I could think to do. I balled my hand into a fist and swung at the bird as hard as I could.

Clock!

I landed a direct hit. The crow sputtered in the air and nose-dived to the ground, but just as it was about to crash, it rose once again. I'd gotten a pretty good shot in, though, and the bird seemed to be flying funny, like one of its wings was damaged.

Before I could jump up to snatch it again, the crow fluttered wonkily into the air, angling to the right. With a few sharp turns, the crow flew off above the trees and out of sight.

The three of us stood there in the stinky air, holding our shirts over our noses.

"Well," Paul said. "That was officially the One and Onlys' first run-in with a robot crow. Everybody okay?"

"Yeah," I said, "but I don't think the crow is. I damaged it a little. Looks like Mr. Nemo is going to have a repair job."

"And if he can't fix it . . . ," Peephole began.

"Nobody can," I finished.

"So, now what?" Peephole asked.

"Now," I said, "we set our sights on Mr. Nemo. It's time to find this big left shoe and learn what all this nonsense is about."

⇒ 8 ⇐

Marshmallows and Hamsters

What do you do when you wake up and the whole world smells like pizza? It's not a trick question: you get pizza.

Well, maybe it wasn't the whole world that smelled like pizza, but all of Bellwood sure seemed to the morning after our dustup with the robot crow. All day at school, people kept sniffing around and talking about what they wanted to put on their pizza. In math class, Eduardo Blackman said his favorite pizza toppings were marshmallows and pineapple. Marty McClusky said you couldn't put those things on a pizza, but Eduardo Blackman said if he couldn't, then how come he did it all the time? For some reason, this really got Marty McClusky going, and then the rest of the class joined in with their opinions, and things went downhill from there. As punishment, Mr. McClelland gave us an impossible math problem about a guy who delivered, like, fifty pizzas and had everybody pay in fractions.

After school, the One and Onlys were set to launch back into the investigation of the robot crow, but we all decided we'd think better on a full stomach. We headed across town to A Pizza Heaven, Bellwood's best and only pizza place, and added ourselves to the growing line of hungry Bellwoodians.

"I still think it's a little weird," Paul said, craning his neck to see to the front of the line.

"It's *super weird*," I said. "I mean, marshmallows on pizza? C'mon!"

"Not that." He shook his head and gestured at the crowd. "Half of Bellwood is here now. And why? Because the town smells like pizza. Doesn't anybody else wonder what's going on?"

"I'm not complaining," Peephole said. "Did you know that once, the entire city of Los Angeles smelled like rotten eggs for days and nobody knew why? I read about it. Things could be a lot worse."

"So why did LA smell like rotten eggs?" Paul asked.

Peephole shrugged. "Don't know. I got nauseous halfway through the article and stopped reading."

"This isn't the first time this has happened," I said. "Remember two days ago, when everybody went to Dr. Dave's for ice cream? The air smelled sweet that day . . . like ice cream."

"But not at Dr. Dave's," Paul said, nodding. "And in fact, that horrible smell the robot crow puffed out yesterday was a lot like the sewer smell that drove people away from Dr. Dave's."

"Don't forget about the rats," Peephole said. "I know I haven't."

An old woman came out the front of A Pizza Heaven. She was wearing a tomato sauce–spattered apron, and her expression was a mix of exhaustion, surprise, and delight. It was Mrs. Lombardi, the owner of the restaurant. She took in the growing crowd and blew a wisp of hair out of her face, then threw her hands up in confusion and walked back into the restaurant. She'd probably never had so many customers at one time in her life.

I looked at Paul. "You think these smells are connected to the robot crow?"

"I'd bet on it," he said. "When two totally unusual things pop up at the same time out of nowhere, odds are, they have something to do with each other."

"You're probably right," I said, "but that sticker on the crow means that Mr. Nemo is behind all of this. If that's true, then just what is he up to?"

Paul stared at the sky, as if the answer might be up there. "We need to get closer to him and observe him. If we shadow him, maybe we'll get some answers."

"Or at least understand where the big left shoe is," Peephole added, "whatever that is."

"Maybe there's a big left shoe somewhere in Bellwood with an answer," I said. "Hey, Peephole, you've got some huge feet. Ever look for a clue in your shoes?"

Peephole blushed. "They're within the normal range for my age group as determined by the American Orthopaedic Association." Peephole was a little sensitive about his big feet. "Besides, if we're looking for big shoes, we should go to Bless Shoes."

"You think Mr. and Mrs. Patel have something to do with this?" Paul asked.

"I'm not ruling anything out," I said.

A voice interrupted us. "I guess everybody else was craving pizza, too, huh?"

We turned around to see my neighbor Dorothea Hightower standing in line behind us. At her side was her little brother, Elvis. He was wearing thick-rimmed glasses and what looked like a kitchen bowl on his head.

"Hey, Dorothea!" I said. "Hey, Elvis. Yeah—you, us, and everyone else in Bellwood." I sniffed. "I guess it's just something in the air."

Dorothea put a hand on her brother's shoulder. "Paul and Peephole, this is Elvis."

"I'm six," Elvis said.

"That's a good age," Paul said appreciatively.

"Guess how old I am," Peephole said.

Elvis sized him up. "Forty-three."

"Close," Peephole said.

"And what about me?" I asked.

Elvis tilted his head, considering. "Five."

"I like your hat," I said, trying not to take his answer personally.

"It's actually not a hat," he said. "It's an invisibility helmet."

"But we can still see you," Peephole said.

"Of course you can," Elvis replied. "It's not turned on. I didn't want to be rude."

"Makes sense," Paul said. "And your glasses are pretty cool, too."

"Thanks, but they're not real glasses."

"Let me guess," Paul said. "X-ray goggles?"

Elvis shook his head carefully. "Don't be silly. They're just plastic. But I think they make me look smart."

"Elvis requested pizza tonight for dinner," Dorothea said. "Actually, he had a huge meltdown about it."

Elvis grinned.

"My parents finally caved in and made me take him here." She waved a hand at the huge crowd. "But I didn't realize all of Bellwood would be here, too."

I scanned the crowd. It might not have been *all* of Bellwood, but it was close. That's the thing about our strange small town: when something—anything—new happens, everybody shows up to see. And when the air reeks of pizza, everybody has the same idea. I recognized just about all the people there. Harmonica Ed was up near the front of the line, blowing out a festive tune on his instrument, and his right-hand man, Flyin' Brian Saucer, shuffled his feet to the beat. A few spots ahead of us were Agnes Wiseacre and her wife, Jill. Agnes was an artist, and her paintings were always up at the art gallery. They were all pretty much the same: portraits of her neighbors' houses, painted as true to life as possible, with one addition—each house had a UFO hovering above it, about to zap it with a laser. I thought her paintings were terrific, but I don't think her neighbors did.

I even caught a glimpse of Mrs. Espinoza, who gave the three of us a sideways glance. I grimaced and wondered if she'd seen us escaping from her yard yesterday.

I wanted to keep discussing the case, but I couldn't with Dorothea and Elvis so near. Rule number one in an investigation is to trust no one. "So," I turned to Dorothea, "how's the social studies project coming along? Did Mayor Pilkington approve your plan to turn the Brewster House into a museum?"

Dorothea's face fell, and she shook her head slowly. "Actually, they're going to turn it into a new restaurant. Part of the New Bellwood project."

"A restaurant?" Paul said, surprised. "But what about the petition? I thought you got all the signatures you needed?"

Dorothea shrugged. "I did, but when I approached him after the assembly the other day, Mayor Pilkington told me the town council had already unanimously approved the new restaurant. In fact, it's supposed to open later this week."

"That's right across the street from our bratwurst truck," Paul said, worry on his face. "That means competition. Do you know what kind of restaurant it will be?"

"Mayor Pilkington didn't say," Dorothea said.

"But what about the house's history?" I asked.

"I guess New Bellwood was more important to them than the past." Dorothea looked up, defeat in her eyes. "There's not much I can do."

I was upset for her, but I realized I didn't have any idea what the place's history *was.* "Why *do* you care so much about the Brewster House?"

"Well, that's kind of complicated." Dorothea looked down at Elvis. "It has to do with the Hightower family history. See, our great-grandpa, James Hightower, came to Bellwood way back in the 1920s, looking for work. He was a carpenter, and he was amazing at making things with his hands. He built most of the furniture in our house. In fact, he helped build a lot of the old buildings in this town, including Town Hall."

"Cool," I said. "Did he help build the Brewster House?"

"No," Dorothea said, "but he did live in it. For a while, at least. It was a rooming house for single men."

"He must have really loved it for you to try to turn it into a museum," Paul said.

Dorothea shook her head. "Oh, no. He hated it,

actually. But it was the only place he could live. Only place he was *allowed* to live."

"What do you mean?" I asked.

Dorothea sighed and hardened her jaw. "My great-grandpa was a skilled worker. A hard worker. He never took the easy way out in his life. He was probably the best carpenter this side of the Mississippi River," she said, raising her chin a little. "But he was Black. And at that time, in Bellwood, that meant that he was treated differently. Worse. The Brewster House was a segregated rooming house. Blacks only. It wasn't as nice or as clean or as big as the other places to stay in Bellwood."

"There was racial segregation in Bellwood?" I asked. We'd learned about racism in school, of course, but I hadn't really thought about *Bellwood* as being part of that history. That kind of thing didn't happen in our little town. But then again . . . I guess it did.

Dorothea nodded. "After a few months passed and his construction jobs were finished, my great-grandpa left Bellwood to find work in other places. He bounced around from town to town, getting short-term jobs and never staying very long. But there was something about Bellwood that he loved, despite the way he had been treated. He helped build it, after all. So he came back many years later, and this time, he was able to buy his own house and start a family."

"Whoa," I said. In fifth grade, we'd learned all about

the history of Bellwood. We'd learned about when it was first settled, and about all the former mayors, and about all the great citizens who made it special. But why hadn't we learned about this? This seemed just as important as that other stuff.

"My great-granddad came to Bellwood in the 1920s, too," Paul said. From the look on his face, he was wondering the same things I was. "I've heard all kinds of stories about him and about Bellwood back then. But I never heard anything about segregation. Isn't that weird?"

"Maybe," Dorothea said, "but your great-granddad had a different experience than mine. Sometimes, if it doesn't happen to somebody directly, they don't think about it or talk about it. But my great-grandpa didn't forget his time at the Brewster House. He told his kids about it, and they told their kids, and my parents told us." She squeezed Elvis's shoulder. "So it's part of *our* story now."

"No wonder you care so much about the place. But . . . if it reminds you and your family of the way your great-grandpa was treated, wouldn't you want to have it demolished? How come you want to turn it into a museum?"

"You said it yourself," Dorothea said enthusiastically. "You didn't know Bellwood had this kind of thing in its past. But people *need* to know. Otherwise, we might be fooled into thinking old Bellwood was perfect. It wasn't. Not for everybody, at least."

"And if something's not perfect," Elvis said, adjusting his glasses, "we should try to fix it."

"We *have* to talk to Mayor Pilkington about this," I said, fired up. "We can't just turn it into another restaurant!"

Dorothea's face fell again. "You can try. But I'm not sure if we can stop it. Honestly, it was nice to see so many people interested in signing the petition. I guess that's a start."

"Maybe Pilkington's here," Peephole said, twisting his head around to search the crowd. He had a better view than any of us. "There he is!"

We followed his gaze to the back of the line. Sure enough, Mayor Pilkington was just arriving, smiling broadly and shaking hands. He clapped the back of a woman with curly hair and pinched her baby's cheeks. He caught Darrel Sullivan, the guy with the bleached goatee, for a handshake even though it looked like Darrel was trying to cross the street in a hurry. Then Pilkington turned to a man with long black hair and thick silver eyebrows.

"Mr. Nemo!" I blurted. "He's *here!*"

Paul and Peephole stood up straight, poised for action.

"I'm gonna tackle him," I announced, but Paul grabbed my arm.

"You can't tackle him now!" Peephole whined.

"You want me to wait until he gets his pizza? C'mon, he's our guy! The sticker, remember?"

"Peephole's right," Paul said. "We've got to shadow him a little. We don't know anything for sure yet."

"Hey," Dorothea said, "are you guys doing one of your mysteries?" For a second, I'd completely forgotten she and Elvis were there. So much for keeping our investigation a secret.

"Oh, yeah . . . but it's sort of hard to explain," I began.

"There's a robot crow on the loose in Bellwood," Paul said. That was his problem: he was too honest. He could have been a truly great detective, but he trusted people way too much.

Dorothea scrunched up her face in confusion.

"*That* robot crow?" Elvis asked, pointing at the roof of A Pizza Heaven.

There it was. Black feathers. Spindly legs. Red eyes. It was perched right on the edge of the roof, just above the Bellwoodians crowding around the door.

Suddenly, its beak hinged open to let out the familiar hissing sound.

"It's doing it again!" Peephole cried. "The spraying thing!"

At that exact moment, I became aware of something moving near my feet. I glanced down to see little bundles of fur scuttling all over.

"Rats!" a frantic voice yelled from the crowd. A panic spread through the line as people hopped up and down in terrified wiggles.

"Actually," Paul said flatly, staring down at the furry critters skittering all around us, "I think they're hamsters."

He was right. Little brown-and-white hamsters were scurrying all through the line. There must have been twenty or more of them. It looked like they had come from inside A Pizza Heaven. They weren't rats, but they were furry and on the loose, so they still caused quite a stir among the crowd.

And then the stench hit. That same rotting stink we'd smelled at Dr. Dave's. The same putrid aroma that the robot crow had sprayed in our faces just the night before.

When I looked back up at the roof of the restaurant, the crow was gone.

"There!" Peephole said, pointing to the sky. The crow was buzzing away, listing to the right. The damaged wing, I remembered. Soon it was out of sight.

"Um, what on earth is going on in Bellwood?" Dorothea asked.

"That's what we're trying to figure out," Paul said.

"How can we help?" she asked.

Paul, Peephole, and I looked at each other. The One and Onlys had always worked alone to solve mysteries. We were a team, and we didn't need anybody else.

"It's another sewer leak!" a voice exclaimed. "All this construction is tearing Bellwood apart!"

An agitated hum went through the crowd, with

people shaking their heads and complaining about all the disruption.

"Attention, everyone! Remain calm!" Mayor Pilkington called out. He was holding his nose and attempting to restore order to the unruly crowd. "I don't know what's going on with the smell or with the . . . hamsters . . . but we'll get this all taken care of! Our crews are doing the best they can, and we're sorry for any inconveniences along the way. But you know what they say—you can't make an omelet without breaking a few eggs."

"Smells like those eggs are rotten," somebody called out.

Mayor Pilkington frowned and raised his hands. "In the meantime, there's a new pizza restaurant just across the street. I know not many of you have visited it yet, but it just so happens that it's part of the New Bellwood project. Do you like innovative food? Then this place will knock your socks off!" Pilkington was slipping into the same New Bellwood speech he'd been giving a lot lately. "Do you like classic wood-fired pizza with an original twist? I hear the salted peanut pizza is a must-have, though I haven't tried it myself . . . nut allergy. Who's hungry? Follow me!" he said, heading across the street toward a building I hadn't even noticed before. It was new and bright. SLICE OF LIFE, the sign read. "The first slice is on me!"

A pleased murmur went through the crowd, and

people followed Mayor Pilkington—Mr. Nemo among them.

I looked back at Dorothea. Maybe she *could* help. She did know an awful lot about Bellwood's history, after all.

"Does the phrase 'big left shoe' mean anything to you?" I asked. It was a long shot, I knew.

Dorothea furrowed her brow and shook her head. "Big left shoe? I don't think—" Her face lit up. "Wait! I know where there's a *really* big shoe. And if I'm not mistaken, I think it's a lefty. . . ."

"Where?" the One and Onlys all asked at once.

"It's one of Bellwood's weirdest and best landmarks. It's actually a project that my great-grandpa worked on. While it lasted, at least. You guys know Wolfgang Munchaus, right?"

Of course we did. He was one of the early mayors of Bellwood. The Bellwood Bratwurst Bonanza was his idea. He was basically the George Washington of Bellwood.

"Did you know he wanted to build an enormous statue of himself welcoming visitors to Bellwood? He had a vision that it would be like the Statue of Liberty, except instead of a torch, he'd be holding a bratwurst."

"That's nuts," Peephole said.

"That's Bellwood," Dorothea replied. "He even drew up blueprints and hired builders. It was going to be one of the modern wonders of the world, according to Mayor Munchaus."

"But I've never seen any giant Munchaus statue," I said.

"That's because they didn't finish it. But my great-grandpa was on the crew that started to build it. In fact, they'd only gotten as far as sculpting Munchaus's left shoe when the project ran out of money and had to be abandoned."

"There's a giant shoe statue in Bellwood?" Paul asked. "Where?"

"It's out in the Bell Woods," Dorothea said. "Way up in the northeastern corner. It was supposed to beckon visitors from far and wide. I'd take you out there now, but I've got to watch Elvis. Sorry I can't help with the mystery."

"Mystery?" Elvis tugged on Dorothea's shirt. "Pizza can wait."

Dorothea looked up at us expectantly. "What do you think?"

"We've got to check out that big left shoe," Paul said. "You lead the way!"

"But what about Nemo?" I objected. "He's right here! Don't we want to get in his face?"

"That's just it," Paul said. "He's here, so we know for certain he's not at the big left shoe. This is the perfect chance to scope it out without him being there. If we find evidence that he's the one behind the robot crow and the smells, then we'll confront him."

Paul was right, as usual. I nodded my agreement, and the three of us hopped on our bikes. Dorothea and Elvis ran to a bike that was leaning against a nearby tree. As Dorothea held it steady, Elvis climbed up and sat on the handlebars, facing forward.

"Is that safe?" Peephole asked, watching them uneasily.

"Not at all," Dorothea said. Elvis shook his head and grinned. "Now let's go find that big shoe!"

They bumped and wavered away from the chaos of the hamsters and the stink, and when they made it to the road, they picked up speed. The One and Onlys followed close behind.

9

The Game Is a Foot

Nobody knew the Bell Woods better than the One and Onlys. We'd spent a lot of time exploring out there among the trees and the fallen logs, and we'd recently moved our secret headquarters into the thick of it. Still, the woods extended from one corner of our town all the way to the other, and so it wasn't shocking that it held a few surprises even for us.

Paul, Peephole, and I followed Dorothea and Elvis as they raced across town and into the woods on an overgrown service road up by Paul's house. We sped as fast as our bikes would carry us, the trees to our sides blurring into a single mass of green. We needed to get to the statue of former Mayor Munchaus's shoe before Mr. Nemo, or whoever else, did.

Along the way, we did our best to fill Dorothea in on

all the details of the investigation. We told her about the smells and the robot crow and Mr. Nemo's sticker under its feathers. She listened intently, leaning her head to the side so she could see around Elvis, who was having the time of his life sitting on the handlebars.

She made a quick right off the service road and into the forest. The One and Onlys followed, bumping and jouncing our way ever deeper into the thicket. Eventually, she slowed down, and we swiveled our heads in search of the strange landmark.

"There!" Peephole thrust a finger straight ahead.

Up ahead, in a clearing where the early-evening sun shone through, was an enormous brown shoe. Dorothea wasn't kidding—as we got closer, more of the bronze statue became visible, and we could finally see how big the shoe was.

"That's the size of a pickup truck!" Peephole said.

"I told you," Dorothea said. "It was supposed to be the tallest thing around for miles."

We hopped off our bikes and stood in the soft grass in front of the biggest piece of footwear I'd ever seen.

"Imagine if they'd built the whole Munchaus," Paul said. "He'd go all the way to the sky."

An engraved plaque at the toe of the shoe read, in bold letters, BEHOLD, YE BRATWURST LOVERS, AND REJOICE! I peered up at the treetops, trying to picture the enormous mayor towering over Bellwood with a bratwurst in his hand. Would it have been an inspiring sight? Or threatening? Or just kind of . . . funny?

"There's something sort of sad about the shoe all by itself out here," Peephole said.

"Sad or not," I said, slowly walking toward it, "it has to hold some answers about our robot crow." The ground in the clearing was softer than the hard dirt of the rest of the woods, and it turned mushy around the unfinished statue. I reached out and touched the shoe. It was cool. I wound up and thwacked it twice. *Gong gong.* "It's hollow," I said, and banged a few more times. "Anybody in there?" No answer came.

"Um, guys?" Peephole called. He popped his head out from the other side of the big shoe. "I think I found something."

"What is it?"

"A door," he said.

We walked across the squishy soil to where Peephole was standing. Sure enough, there, on the back heel of Munchaus's shoe, was a small doorknob.

"Here goes nothing," I said, then turned the knob and pushed the door open.

The light from outside shone in to reveal a small room. There was a chair, slightly askew, in front of a table with nothing on it but a battery-powered lantern. Tacked to the wall above the table was what looked like a map, and under the table sat a black box.

"Munchaus used his shoe as an office?" Peephole asked.

Paul shook his head. "This stuff was added recently."

We walked across the small room. I reached down and pulled up the black box, surprised to find it was so light. I put it on the table and lifted the lid. Empty.

"Do you think this is where the robot crow lives?" Dorothea asked.

"Maybe," Paul said. "But it's not here now."

"What's this map?" I asked, leaning closer to inspect it.

"It's Bellwood," Peephole said. "But a few locations are highlighted." He tapped on various points of the map that had been marked with a pen. "This star here is where Butter Baby's House of Shakes is."

"And look, there's an *X* right across the street," Dorothea said. "That must be—"

"Dr. Dave's," Paul said. "And here's another star, right at the new pizza place, Slice of Life."

"And an *X* over the spot for A Pizza Heaven," I said. "I'm beginning to see a pattern here. . . ."

"Uh-oh," Peephole said. He tapped the center of the map, representing the very center of Bellwood.

"That's the Brewster House," Dorothea said. "And there's another *X* across the street."

"That's our bratwurst truck!" Paul said, a fierce look in his eyes.

"So the stars are the new restaurants," I said, "part of the New Bellwood project. And the X's are the old places."

"The places where the robot crow let out its epic stink," Peephole said. "What is Mr. Nemo trying to do?"

"Isn't it obvious?" Paul scowled. "The crow flies all over town, spraying alluring smells. People crave ice cream, then pizza, and they head to their old favorite restaurants. But while they're waiting in line, the crow spits out a stink bomb that drives people away—"

"And directly to the newly opened restaurants across the street, specializing in the exact same food," I said.

"And can we please not forget the rats," Peephole added.

"Or the hamsters," I said.

We stared at the map. The big X's didn't lie. The Brewster House and Paul's parents' bratwurst truck were targets. This case had become personal.

"The rats make sense," Paul said. "I mean, you can imagine that maybe they came from the restaurant. But hamsters are just"—he shook his head—*"weird."*

He pulled his phone out of his back pocket and started thumbing it excitedly.

"What are you doing?" I asked.

"I'm looking up the new restaurants. Maybe there's something about them online. I'll start with Butter Baby's. . . ."

Peephole and I crowded over Paul's phone. The

search came back with a map with little red dots all over it. They were the locations of Butter Baby's restaurants.

"It's a chain?" I said, surprised.

"Looks like there are locations all over the state," Paul said. He tapped another search out.

"And Slice of Life is a chain, too." I read the results. "Over four hundred locations nationwide."

"If there's four hundred of them, why do they need another in Bellwood?" Paul said.

"New Bellwood," Dorothea said sadly.

"Something major is happening here," I said. "But I can't quite figure out what it is."

"Bozo!" Elvis shouted.

"Hey, I just need a little time to think about it," I said defensively, but then I saw that Elvis had found something under the table.

It was an empty Bozo bar wrapper.

Elvis lifted it to his nose and sniffed. "Chocolaty."

"If it still smells, that means somebody's been here recently," Paul said.

"Very recently," Peephole said, bending down to look at the floor.

"Footprints!" I said, amazed that we'd been too distracted by the table and the map to notice the muddy shoeprints.

"Fresh ones," Peephole said. "The mud is still wet."

"Somebody must have left right before we got here!"

I said. We scampered outside to look for any prints that weren't ours.

"Here!" Paul said, crouch-walking over a fresh line of tracks leading out of the shoe and through the clearing toward the service road. Where they reached the end of the clearing and the ground became hard again, the prints disappeared.

"Whoever this was," Peephole said, measuring the prints against his, "they have smaller feet than me."

"That could be half of Bellwood," I said. "No offense," I added, noticing Peephole's defensive look.

"No, it couldn't," Paul said. "Remember what Mr. Nemo said about the Bozo bars? The vending machine in the rec center is the only place in town that has them."

"So, whoever this was, they've been at the rec center recently?" Dorothea asked.

"All signs are pointing to Nemo," Paul said.

We stood there in silence for a few seconds, letting the evidence settle in. The fading sun glinted off the bronze of the giant shoe in the clearing. If that monument was any clue, old Bellwood was a strange place. Then again, New Bellwood was proving to be just as odd.

10

Pulling the Plug

"Mr. Nemo is on his way here, so we don't have much time to figure out how we want to confront him about the crow and the smells and the big shoe in the woods," I said, leading Paul, Peephole, and Dorothea to the corner of the crowded cafeteria where the vending machine stood. "My vote is, we wait until he's not looking and tackle him."

"First of all," Peephole said, "your vote is always to tackle people. And second . . . what do you mean, Mr. Nemo is on his way here? To the middle school? To lunch?"

"To this vending machine, to be precise," I said, patting the side of the machine. "I called him up right before our lunch period. I said the vending machine in the cafeteria was broken and he needed to come fix it. So he'll be here any minute."

"You called him up?" Dorothea asked, grinning. "That's so gutsy. You guys are pretty good at this detective thing, aren't you?"

"Gutsy is my middle name," I said, blushing slightly at the compliment.

"I thought your middle name was Longshanks," Peephole said.

"It is," I said. We stared at each other for a long moment.

"But what if he's suspicious that a kid called him about the school's machine?" Paul asked.

"He doesn't know I'm a kid," I said. "I called from school office."

"You *what*?" Peephole gasped.

I shrugged. "I passed the office on my way to lunch and stopped in. Told the lady at the desk that I needed to call my mom and could I borrow the phone? She said sure. So I turned my back to her and called Nemo instead. His phone registered a call from Bellwood Middle School, so he doesn't know any different."

"That's so cool," Dorothea said admiringly. "But what's he going to say when four kids are waiting here for him?"

"We're not waiting for him," I said slyly. "We're just some kids who are disappointed because the vending machine isn't working."

"But it is working," Peephole said, sending a dollar

into the slot and pressing the buttons for a Slap-of-Wack bar. The insides of the machine hummed, and the bar dropped with a small thud.

"You're right," I said. "We have to break it."

"We can't break it!" Peephole protested.

"Don't look now," Paul said, "but Mrs. Espinoza is watching us."

I ignored Paul's instruction and looked. There she was, in the corner of the lunchroom, giving us the side-eye.

"She seems pretty suspicious of us," Dorothea said. "Does she always look at you guys like that?"

"Pretty much, actually," I said. Last time we'd talked to Mrs. Espinoza, she'd said it seemed like we were always hiding something. I guess I had to admit that she was right.

I swiveled away from her and lowered my voice. "This is it, guys. This is our chance to nail him and get some answers. Did you forget about Mr. Nemo's little map in Munchaus's shoe?" I looked at Dorothea. "Remember the star on the Brewster House?" I turned to Paul. "And the *X* over the Honest Bratwurst truck? We *have* to do something about this. If we don't, who will? This is about more than just a stupid robot bird. It's about Bellwood. It's about our *families*. Come *on*," I urged, my voice a little louder than I meant it to be. "We can't back down now."

Paul looked like he was about to protest, but he paused. He was cautious by nature, but he knew I was right about the bratwurst truck. Whatever was happening with the crows and the smells, it didn't look good for the old restaurants in Bellwood. Especially his parents' place.

"She's right," Dorothea said.

Paul nodded slowly.

"He's here!" Peephole whispered. "Nemo!"

We swung our heads to look across the cafeteria. Mr. Nemo's pitch-black ponytail swished behind him as he walked. Seeing him weaving his way, toolbox gripped in one hand, through the chaos of middle-school lunch, I realized just how old he was. His small, bent body marched through the sea of flailing arms and legs and Tater Tots like he was a man on a mission. And he was. A mission to fix the vending machine. Too bad it wasn't broken.

"I'm going to pull the plug," I said. "Help me move this thing so I can reach it." I gripped the side of the machine and started pushing, but it wouldn't budge.

"That's the plan?" Peephole said, not moving to help. "It'll take him two seconds to figure out there's nothing wrong with it."

"Doesn't matter," I grunted. "The plan was to get him here. Now start pushing."

Next to me, Paul leaned into the machine, too, and the

two of us pushed with all our might. Dorothea joined us, and finally Peephole lent his weight. At last, the vending machine budged, but only a few inches. Still, the plug was in sight.

"Ahem."

The voice came from behind us. We turned to see Mrs. Espinoza, arms folded, staring down at us. She didn't look impressed by our amazing feat of team strength.

"Going somewhere with that?" She flicked her head at the machine.

"Of course not," I said quickly. "We were just . . ."

Usually, I had no problem coming up with a quick cover story. But this time, Mrs. Espinoza's gaze was sort of unnerving. I drew a blank.

"There it is!" Dorothea suddenly said, pointing at the floor behind the vending machine. I didn't see anything, but she crouched down and reached to the floor. When she stood back up, there was a little silver ring in her hand. "My mom would have *killed* me if I'd lost my great-grandma's ring. It's been in the family for generations." She smiled at Peephole, Paul, and me. "Thanks again for helping me find it. You guys are the best."

Peephole looked confounded. "Well, we actually didn't—"

"No problem at all," I said, cutting him off, realizing that Dorothea was handling the cover story.

"Mrs. Espinoza?" Dorothea said, turning to our

social studies teacher. "Do you have a minute? I just have a couple of questions that I wanted to ask you about our project."

"Well, sure," Mrs. Espinoza said.

"Great!" Dorothea began walking away from the vending machine, and Mrs. Espinoza followed at her side. "I'm researching the Brewster House, remember? And well, I've come across some interesting information. . . ."

When they were a few steps away, Dorothea cast a glance over her shoulder and winked at us. Thanks to her, we were clear to talk to Mr. Nemo alone.

"That was smooth," Peephole said.

I scurried to the back of the machine, gripped the thick cord, and yanked it. The machine went silent and its buttons went dark.

And then we turned to face Mr. Nemo, emerging from the crowd toward us. We did our best to pretend we weren't watching him. At least, I did. I tapped on the clear plastic of the machine and acted like it had eaten my dollar. Peephole stared right at him.

"Pardon me, kids," he said in that familiar whispering tone, stopping in front of the vending machine and setting his toolbox on the floor. "I got a report that this puppy's tail's not wagging anymore."

"Huh?" Peephole said.

"The vending machine is broken," Mr. Nemo said. "At least, I got a phone call that said so."

"Yeah," I said, giving the machine a little kick. "These things are always breaking down, huh? But I guess that's why they called you. You can fix anything. Right? And make just about anything? I bet you've made some crazy things in your day, huh? What's the weirdest thing you ever made?"

Mr. Nemo looked down at me for the first time. His silver eyebrows framed his wrinkled eyes, which were still bright. He flashed them over to Paul, then up to Peephole. "I know you," he said, pointing his finger at me. "The detectives, right?" I was expecting to see the usual look we get from adults when they learn we're a detective team—a laugh, or a smirk, or an isn't-that-cute lip pucker—but Mr. Nemo just nodded. He seemed to take us seriously.

"The One and Onlys," I said, with a little bow. "In fact, we're still working on the case we told you about. Remember? The one about the robot crow? Making progress on it, actually."

Mr. Nemo tipped his head slowly, still fixing me with his narrow eyes.

"A lot of progress," I added, staring right back at him.

Without having to see them, I could feel Paul and Peephole giving me a look. It was the easy-does-it look that I got about a hundred times during an investigation. And I knew they were probably right. We probably *should* have eased up a little bit and waited for more evidence, but the truth was that I was impatient. Here was Mr. Nemo, our prime (and only) suspect in the robot crow shenanigans, and he was standing right next to us. We could *observe* him all we wanted, but while we did that, his robot crow was flying all over town and blasting horrible sprays in people's faces. The most important rule of sleuthing is that patience is overrated.

"In fact," I continued, "we got hold of the robot crow. For a little while, at least. And we found some interesting evidence on it. Want to know what we found?"

Mr. Nemo glanced back up at the vending machine and sighed. He was silent for a moment, then turned to look over his shoulder at the madness of the cafeteria. "Been a long time since I've been in this building. Hasn't changed much. Isn't that funny?" He chuckled to himself and shook his head. "Seems like the world has made itself over a few times since I was a kid here, but this room"—he swept out a hand at the noise of rowdy Bellwoodian middle schoolers—"it still sounds the same. Maybe that's one thing that never changes."

"I don't know about that," I said, trying to control my adrenaline, "but I was talking about the robot crow."

He gazed down at me. "There's something about you, isn't there?"

I stared right back at him. "What's that supposed to mean?"

"Something different," he replied. Then, abruptly, he held up a finger and turned his back to us. He picked up his toolbox and moved a few steps away. I wondered for a second if he was going to try and make a run for it, which wouldn't have been much of a problem. After all, the first rule of solving mysteries is to always be ready for a chase. But he looked back at us and whispered, "Follow me. I have a couple of things I want to show you."

Paul and Peephole looked at me, waiting for me to protest. But I had to admit that I was curious, so I followed Mr. Nemo. He walked slowly out of the lunchroom, leading us partway down a hallway with a glass case I'd passed every day this week on the way to lunch. It was filled with plaques and pictures and trophies from the past. Mr. Nemo stopped in front of the case and put his tools down again. "There." He pointed. "See that?"

We followed his pointing finger to an old black-and-white photograph in the back of the case. It was of a kid, maybe our age, with thick black hair and eyebrows, wearing white tights and smiling broadly, a medal around his neck. A stern-looking bald man with glasses and a thin mustache stood behind him, a hand on his shoulder.

"Who's that?" Paul asked.

"Read the caption," Mr. Nemo said.

We leaned closer to the glass, squinting to read the caption below the framed photograph. I read it out loud: "'1952 State Gymnastics Champion Marvin Nemo Jr. poses with his medal. Proud coach—and father—Marvin Nemo Sr. looks on.' That's you? You're Marvin?"

Mr. Nemo nodded. "And my dad. He came from a

different generation—one that didn't smile for pictures." He gazed at the picture intently, as if the boy and his father might spring to life at any moment. "He was a very hard man to please. My whole life, I tried to make him proud of me. Or maybe I was always afraid of disappointing him. But you can't always please everybody, can you? After all, it's your life. I figured that out, eventually. Anyway, I knew he was proud of me, this once, for being state champion. He never said it in those words, exactly, but I could just feel it. This was one of my happiest days."

"Wow," Paul said. "You weren't kidding about it being a long time since you'd been here."

"This is interesting and all," I said, "but . . . why are you showing it to us?"

He turned to us and heaved another sigh. "I've lived in Bellwood my whole life. My friends are here. My work is here. My memories are all here. I've repaired or given life to a thousand machines up and down these streets. I'm proud to call myself a Bellwoodian. And you have to understand that I would never do anything to harm the town."

"But," I blurted impatiently, "what about the—"

"Robot crow?" he said, surprising me. "You found my sticker on it, right?"

Paul and Peephole stood there, stunned, staring at Mr. Nemo. They were speechless that he'd admitted it.

I wasn't. "You better believe we found the sticker," I said. "How can you explain that?"

"Easy." He shrugged. "I made them."

"You did?" Peephole asked. "I mean, you're *admitting* you did?"

"I *knew* it!" I said. "But . . . what do you mean, 'them'?"

"There's two of them," Mr. Nemo rasped. "But it's not what you think. I saw you at the pizza restaurant yesterday. And I know that you saw the robot crow there. I saw it, too. And I saw what it did. Or I should say, I *smelled* what it did."

"Because you programmed it that way!" I said.

Mr. Nemo shook his head. "I said there was another thing I wanted to show you." He bent down and clicked his toolbox open, pulling out an envelope. He gripped it close to his chest for a moment, then handed it to me.

"What is this?" I asked.

"Read it."

I pulled a thick piece of cream-colored stationery from the envelope. The bottom corners were rounded, but the top corners were right angles, and the paper seemed a little shorter than a typical piece. On it was a short hand-written message and a drawing.

Dear Mr. Nemo, You say you can make anything. Can you make this? I need two remote-controlled drones that can fly long-range. They need to be quiet—silent, if possible. And they need to look like a crow. Here's a little something to get you started. If you can do it, leave them hidden in a box in the bushes by the red maple in Munchaus Park in one week. Once I receive the crows, you'll get another payment.

Below the message was a simple drawing of a crow, marked up with a small list of instructions.

Beak needs to open and shut.

Built-in camera for remote viewing and control.

Long battery life.

Must look REAL.

"Who sent this to you?" I asked.

"I wish I knew," Mr. Nemo said. "They didn't sign it. It arrived in my mailbox without a return address. Inside was . . . a lot of cash."

"So you made them? Weren't you curious?" Paul asked.

"Of course I was. I've made some odd things for people—once I modified a guy's toaster so that it was safe to put his socks and underwear in it—but this one took the cake. I had no idea what they were going to use it for. How could I have?" He glanced over at the picture of himself as a kid. "Besides, it was a challenge. And I like challenges."

"But what about the stink sprayer?" Peephole asked. "Didn't you think *that* was weird?"

He shook his head. "I didn't have anything to do with that. Whoever asked for this must have added that feature later."

"When you dropped the crows off in the bushes in the park, did you see anybody?" Paul asked.

"No," Mr. Nemo said thoughtfully, "but there *was*

something unusual about that. I put the crows in the spot like the letter asked me to, and I even gave the money back. Like I said, I did it for the challenge alone. Then I stopped in the public restroom before I left the park. I couldn't have been in there for more than two minutes, but I began to worry the crows weren't tucked under the bushes enough. So when I came out, I walked back over to the bushes to hide the box better, but it was already gone."

"Somebody came and snatched it up that quickly?" Paul asked.

"They must have been hiding somewhere in the park, because there wasn't another soul in sight," Mr. Nemo said. "The next day, as promised, another wad of cash arrived in my mailbox. To be honest, I didn't think much of it. And then you kids mentioned the robot crow at the rec center the other night. But it wasn't until I saw it myself at A Pizza Heaven last night—saw that it caused the whole crowd to flee—that I realized something was wrong."

"Does the letter give us any clues?" Paul asked. I handed it over to him, and he held it up. The small, cursive writing was smudged a little, but it was still neat and legible.

"That's the same handwriting as on the crow sticker," Peephole said. "See? Same looping *p* and slanted *e*."

I had to take Peephole's word for it. I never would

have noticed that in a million years, but then again, Peep-hole has a photographic memory. It's like he can take pictures with his mind and revisit them in perfect detail whenever he wants. Sometimes it's a curse, like when Jacob Perkins drank six cherry slushies during lunch and then barfed from the top of the rope in gym class so that it splashed down hot red rain on everybody below. Sometimes, though, it did come in handy during a case.

Paul held the paper up against the light. "Aha!" he exclaimed. "Just as I expected. This is nice stationery, and that sometimes means there's a watermark!"

"A what?" I asked.

"You know, like a symbol you can only see when you hold the paper a certain way. This letter's got one!"

We all scrunched together to look at the watermark.

"Is that . . . a drawing of a—"

"Crow!" I practically shouted. It was hard to make out at first, but once I saw it, it was unmistakable. The faint watermark was a tiny outline of a crow.

"Oh, no," Peephole groaned. "They've got fancy paper. That means they're important. This is not good."

"This is *great*!" I said. "A clue is a clue. We're getting closer to finding our culprit." I turned to Mr. Nemo. "I guess you don't know anything about what's inside Mayor Munchaus's giant left shoe out in the corner of the Bell Woods?" I asked.

Mr. Nemo cocked his head to the right, confused.

"Didn't think so."

"You know what this means?" Paul said, turning to us. "If Mr. Nemo isn't the one who's been operating the crow from the shoe, then somebody else who's been eating Bozo bars is. And that means they've been at the rec center."

"Maybe they're a member of the Lyrical Warriors!" I said.

"I'd bet on it," Paul said.

"And if they are, then we're that much closer to catching them!" I said. "Mr. Nemo, can you do us a favor? Can you keep this conversation between us? Whoever is doing all this stuff, we want to make sure we keep the element of surprise."

Mr. Nemo zipped up his lips. "No problem. I'm good at keeping secrets." Then he snapped his fingers and pointed at me. "I figured out what's special about you," he said. "You're fearless, aren't you?"

"Guilty as charged," I said. *Well, that used to be true,* I thought. But if I was truly that brave, then how come my knees got weak every time I thought about climbing something tall? Still, I needed to keep up appearances. "Fear is just something you've got to move out of the way to get what you want."

"That's a good philosophy, I think," Mr. Nemo said.

"Tell that to my dad," I muttered.

"Oh?" Mr. Nemo said. "He doesn't trust you?"

"If it were up to him, he'd cover me in Bubble Wrap every time I left the house."

"Don't see eye to eye with your old man, huh?" Mr. Nemo turned back to the picture of himself and his dad. "Looks like we've got that much in common." He let out a big breath, bent down to pick up his toolbox, and turned to us. "Well, that's all I know. I have to say, I'm glad that you're on the case. With a few capable detectives tracking down clues, this ought to be solved in no time. You three have your work cut out for you. If anything breaks during your investigation . . ."

"We know," Paul said. "Give you a call."

Mr. Nemo winked. "Be careful, will you? This whole crow business could be dangerous." He turned to go. "Oh, and one last thing," he said over his shoulder as he walked back toward the cafeteria.

"What?"

"Plug the vending machine back in. It works better that way."

→ 11 ←

Wrestling with Changes

I rolled my bike out of our driveway and picked up speed on the open stretch of road. Standing up on the pedals and leaning over the handlebars, I felt my long hair flow behind me as my eyes teared up from the wind in my face. The sun was just starting to slide down the sky to my right, and for the first time since spring, I felt the tiniest chill in the air. It was late summer, after all, or early fall, depending on who you asked, and it felt like the weather was changing. Actually, it felt like all of Bellwood was changing.

Another Thursday night meant another Lyrical Warriors Poetry Wrestling Club meeting at the rec center. As always, the One and Onlys would meet up there, but this time, we wouldn't just be watching from the sidelines. We'd be sniffing out suspects. Whoever was controlling the robot crow, or *crows*, from the statue of Munchaus's shoe had eaten a Bozo bar, which they could only have gotten from the vending machine in the rec center. I had a hunch that the culprit must be a Lyrical Warrior. But who?

I'd asked my parents if I could ride my bike and meet them there. The rec center was nestled near the center of Bellwood, right next to the elementary school, but I was planning on taking a meandering route. The journey would give me time to sort out in my head some of the details of the Case of the Robot Crow, and it would also be an opportunity to swing by Munchaus Park and look for any clues as to who might have picked up the package Mr. Nemo left there.

It felt good to go fast. Racing on my bike was uncomplicated. It wasn't confusing. If you pumped your legs, you would go fast, and unlike Peephole, I liked going fast. It calmed me down. The faster I went and the blurrier the world around me got, the more at peace I felt.

But as I whipped down Radford, I was distracted by the changes to the street. They were small changes, mostly unnoticeable if you weren't looking for them, but since I knew every street and corner of Bellwood, anything new jumped out at me. First were the streetlamps. They had been installed only in the last week or so, and they were bright and silvery and hung like question marks over the road. Then the grass. It was green. Like, really, really green. Probably because of the new town-wide sprinkler system that sprayed water on all city land every hour. And then the new signs, which seemed to be everywhere. Signs showing the speed limit, signs flashing for a crosswalk, signs thanking you for not littering. I didn't know what New Bellwood would be like, exactly, but I knew there would be a lot of signs.

Up ahead, I caught a glimpse of Butter Baby's and the enormous milkshake rotating on its roof. Lit up in neon, it seemed to attract me to it like I was a bug and it was a lightbulb. Across the street, Dr. Dave's Ice Cream Parlor looked small and run-down in comparison.

After I passed Butter Baby's, the Conquistador megastore jutted up from the earth in the southwest corner of Bellwood like a bright, sleek monster. It was twice as new and twice as tall as any other building around it, and at least four times as wide. In the daytime, its gleaming orange and red paint reflected the sunlight so that it was hard to look at. Right now, with the sun slipping down into the Bell Woods behind it, the windows seemed almost black.

Finally, near the bottom of Bellwood, I steered my bike to the left, and the sun at my back gave everything in front of me a rosy glow. I slowed my pace as I passed Munchaus Park. It was a small park—just a field, a bike path, a few clusters of trees with benches, and a public restroom—and so it was never that crowded. The perfect spot for the shady exchange of weird robot birds, I guess. I rolled nearly to a stop, spotting the red maple and bushes that Mr. Nemo must have been talking about. Swinging my gaze all over the park, I didn't see anything that looked like a clue. A lady was out on the field, listening to headphones and practicing her kickboxing form, giving the invisible person in front of her a hard time. A couple of little kids were playing tag on the path, slapping each other on the back and arguing over who was really "it."

I thought of what Mr. Nemo had said about the crows being gone after a couple of minutes. Whoever took them must have been hiding nearby. I scanned the park and saw a few likely spots—a bench to crouch behind, a tree to sit in, a bush or two—but not much else. Across the street, a flag fluttered in front of Town Hall, and across the other street, the sunlight was reflected in the windows of a few houses and a white delivery truck. If there was something here that would crack the case open, I didn't see it.

From the park, I zipped back up north past the old water tower, officially the tallest thing in Bellwood. I'd always wanted to climb it, but now, for some reason, the sight of it sent a little shiver down my back, and I remembered the weightless feeling of falling—just for a second—from Funston's Oak. The shiver faded as I pumped away from the tower, but the memory of the fall lingered.

I arrived at the rec center just as the Lyrical Warriors meeting was about to start, and there was a small traffic jam at the door. Tania Rose had just driven Mayor Pilkington up to the door in the lime-green golf cart, and the mayor hopped out and insisted that all the citizens of Bellwood enter before him. Mrs. Espinoza thanked him and passed by, followed by a lady in an animal costume—maybe a ferret?—and a guy with a glittery blue mask and a hairy chest, drinking a Butter Baby's milkshake.

When I reached the door, I said, "Thanks, Mr. Mayor."

"No sweat at all . . ." He squinted at me, clearly trying to remember my name.

"Gloria Hill," Tania whispered over his shoulder. "Daughter of Wes and Estelle."

"People call me Shanks," I said.

"No sweat, Shanks." Pilkington winked, then followed me inside.

Paul, Peephole, and Trillium were already in our usual spot in the front row. Sitting next to them were Dorothea and Elvis, the newest additions to our team. As I made my way across the rec center, I passed a familiar face seated in the back row.

"Vending machine broken again?" I asked.

Mr. Nemo smiled, his silver eyebrows poking up. "Not as far as I know," he said. "No, I'm just here as a spectator tonight. Our conversation this afternoon inspired me to get out and try something new."

I pointed a thumb at the ring. "Ever wrestle before?"

"Looks dangerous," Mr. Nemo rasped.

"Most things worth doing are," I said, then flipped him a wave and crossed over to my friends.

Peephole was wearing some kind of smock, and I knew right away it was to protect him from Trillium's spit-ups.

"I'm not taking any chances tonight," he said, noticing my reaction as I sat down.

"I think it's a good look for you," I said. "Paul, pass the cheese puffs."

"All right, team," Paul began, grabbing a last handful before handing the bag over to me, "let's think about this logically. A robot crow shows up in Bellwood. It's able to fly all over town, completely undetected, perching wherever it wants—"

"And spraying aromas, both delicious and disgusting, out of its beak," I said, stuffing my mouth with cheese puffs.

"Whoever is behind this got Mr. Nemo to build the crows for them, but they were careful to keep their identity hidden. So let's say the crows' scents are meant to lure people to restaurants, then send them fleeing to the New Bellwood places across the street."

"And let's not forget the X on your parents' truck."

"And whoever has been controlling the crow has been operating in secret, from a control room inside the statue of Munchaus's shoe in the Bell Woods," Dorothea said.

"And they have fancy paper," Peephole added.

"*And* most importantly, that person is probably in this room right now," Paul said.

The four of us cast our eyes around. Paul was right. The culprit was likely among us, but we still didn't have enough evidence to determine who it was. At this very moment, there were twenty or so suspects flopping around the rec center.

"Just imagine," Dorothea said, an excited grin on her face, "what Mayor Munchaus would say if he saw what was happening in Bellwood these days. New restaurants, new buildings, robots flying around the skies."

"Do you think he'd recognize his town at all?" Paul asked.

"Hard to say," Dorothea said. "In some ways, it would probably seem like a brand-new place. But other things haven't changed much at all, I bet."

"Have you ever wanted to invent a time machine to go back and spend a day in old Bellwood?" I asked. "Maybe go to the first Bellwood Bratwurst Bonanza?"

"It would be fascinating to see what it was *really* like," Dorothea said, but her smile faded. "But I don't think it would be a great idea."

"Because you might tear a hole in the space-time continuum?" Peephole asked.

"That," Dorothea said, "and Wolfgang Munchaus was mayor in the 1930s. I don't think I'd have been too comfortable back then."

I remembered what Dorothea had said about her great-grandfather—how he had been forced to stay at the Brewster House because it was the only rooming house in town that allowed Black people. Of course Dorothea wouldn't have felt comfortable back then. She couldn't have done a lot of the things we were doing. It would have been against the law. It wasn't fair, and I wanted to say that to her. But Dorothea already knew it.

"I'm sorry," I said, because I couldn't think of anything better. "I feel bad."

"It's not *your* fault," she replied. "You weren't there."

"I know, but I still feel kind of . . . guilty."

"You shouldn't." Dorothea shook her head. "And the museum . . . I don't want to create it to make people feel guilty. But they should know that Bellwood's past is . . . complicated, like anywhere else's. There were great people, and great things happened here. But also some not-so-great stuff. Both of those things can be true, and if we know that and can talk about it, then we can make sure that Bellwood's future will be even better for everyone. But I know what you mean when you say you're sorry. Thanks for saying it."

We sat in silence for a minute, watching the Lyrical Warriors. It was a funny mix of people. There was

Darrel Sullivan, and the Marconis, and the Patels, and Mr. Nemo, and Tania Rose, and the guy in the blue mask—whoever he was. They were all Bellwoodians, but that probably meant something different to each of them. I was starting to see that maybe Mrs. Espinoza had been right: there wasn't just one story of Bellwood, there were all kinds.

"I bet those 1930s bratwursts tasted good, though," Dorothea said, the grin returning.

"Guess what's the biggest food I've ever eaten," Elvis said, jumping out of his seat to face everybody.

Before we could answer, he showed us. "I ate a hot dog that was this long." He spread his arms out as wide as he could, almost losing his balance in the process.

"Wow," Paul said appreciatively. "That's impressive."

"The whole thing," Elvis added. "I had a stomachache for a month."

Dorothea looked at us and nodded her head slightly to confirm that it was true.

"So, where do we begin?" Peephole asked, turning his attention back to the crowd.

"Let's think about motive," Paul said. "Who would want to sabotage the old restaurants and draw people to the new ones?"

"New Bellwood is Mayor Pilkington's project," Peephole replied. "There's a lot of pressure for it to be a success. Maybe he's behind it."

"That's a clear motive." Paul nodded. "But do you really think the mayor could mastermind this whole thing? Did you see him at the assembly? He's out to lunch most of the time."

"It could be an act," I said.

"I will not go gentle into that good bite!" Mayor Pilkington shrieked from the ring, then charged toward my dad, who, from behind, was a dead ringer for the Specter. Once he moved, though, you could tell the difference. My dad tried to bolt out of the way, but he tripped on his cape, tearing it clean off the rest of his costume. Mayor Pilkington tumbled over my dad, then dived through the ring ropes, taking flight on a path bound for the front row.

There was a chunky boom, some rattling, lots of scrapes, and a series of *oof*s and *owf*s as Mayor Pilkington crashed into the seats. He staggered to his feet and started to straighten the chairs around him. "Is everyone okay?" he asked, though nobody was near him. "A mayor's first responsibility is to his citizens!"

Tania Rose swooped in, dusted the mayor off, and pointed him back in the direction of the ring.

"Okay, it would have to be one *heck* of an act," I admitted. "Who else, then? What about him?"

I pointed at a tall bald man up in the ring, practicing what looked like some kind of bird walk with long, stalking steps and flapping arms. I recognized him as the fastidious manager of the Conquistador, obsessed with keeping the store clean. He stopped mid-stride, hopped out of the ring, and kicked some clutter out of the way. "Need a clear space to walk," I heard him say. "Need to keep these aisles clean!"

"Tall people are usually quite trustworthy," Peephole said. "What about Mrs. Newsome?"

"The poetry teacher?" I glanced over to Mrs. Newsome, who was seated in the front row. Her leg was stretched out in a cast, and it had been that way since her unsuccessful attempt at a diving moonsault leg drop at the first meeting of the Lyrical Warriors. Since then, she'd sat on her perch and offered critiques of the members' poetry.

"Couldn't be," Paul said. "According to Mr. Nemo, the robot was taken from the hiding spot in a matter of minutes. Because of her injured leg, she wouldn't have been able to swoop in and get it that quickly."

"Good point. So, who else?" I asked, scanning the room. I locked eyes with Mrs. Espinoza, our social studies teacher, who was peering at us from the corner by the vending machine, and again I had the feeling she was suspicious of us. But for the first time, we weren't doing anything wrong. Still, she began walking our way, and I tensed up.

"Making any progress?" she asked, standing in between us and the ring.

"Um, on what?" I asked.

"Your social studies project. Aren't you researching this very building?" She twisted around to showcase the rec center.

"Oh, uh, yeah. Well, actually, the rec center is sort of the background for my project. I'm really focusing in on the disappearance of the Specter."

"I see," she said. "And have you solved that mystery yet?"

"Well . . . no," I said truthfully. I hadn't done much thinking about the Specter. "But I'm planning on interviewing Mr. Patel about it tonight," I added, making that up out of thin air. "He was there, you know. I *will* get to the bottom of it. The first rule of solving mysteries is to stay with it no matter what."

Mrs. Espinoza nodded, apparently satisfied, and turned her attention to my friends. "I know that you are hard at work on this project, Dorothea. What about you, Paul? Aren't you learning about your family's hardware store?"

"That's right." Paul nodded. "I interviewed my grandpa, which was really cool. He helped his dad build it back in the 1950s. It's the only—I mean, it *used* to be the only place in town to get hardware, so my grandpa had all kinds of stories about helping everybody in Bellwood. It seems like everybody knew everybody in those days."

"Times have changed," she agreed. "How about you, Peephole?"

Peephole shifted Trillium to his other shoulder and

looked up at Mrs. Espinoza. "I'm getting taller, I know that. But I'm not sure how else I'm changing."

Mrs. Espinoza cracked a grin. "I mean, did you ever decide what your project would be about?"

Peephole looked momentarily panicked, and I thought it might be him instead of Trillium who puked—at least he had the smock—but he swallowed hard and nodded his head. "Yeah, actually. I'm going to be writing about the unfinished Wolfgang Munchaus statue. Did you know about it? Ever been there?"

Clever move, I thought. *If everybody here is a suspect, then so is Mrs. Espinoza.* I watched her reaction carefully.

"A Wolfgang Munchaus statue?" she said, with a little shake of her head. "That's news to me, but it sounds perfect for the project. Looks like I'll be learning quite a bit in a week's time!"

She pivoted and walked away, leaving me to contemplate just how far behind I was on my homework. Luckily, Mr. Patel appeared at that very moment from the bathroom, and I waved to catch his attention.

"Size three red high-tops?" he called, straightening his orange jumpsuit as he approached us.

"That's me, but Shanks is a lot easier to say," I said. "Mr. Patel, you mentioned—"

"Arjun, please."

"Arjun. Remember when you said you'd been here at the rec center the night that the Specter disappeared?

I'm doing a project on him, and I'd love to hear more about it."

"June 15, 1962. I remember it like it was yesterday," he said, a breezy smile forming on his lips. "The Specter was . . . *amazing*. Hands down the greatest athlete I've ever seen in my life. I'll tell you something. I've always known I wanted to sell shoes for a living, even as a kid, but—"

"Really?" I said.

"Of course—doesn't every kid? But watching the Specter up there made me want to be a wrestler. Those moves . . . it was like he was ice-skating in the ring."

I tried to imagine what it must have been like to see the Specter in person. I looked up at the ring and watched my dad, whose costume was a nearly exact replica of the Specter's, except that my dad's cape had torn off. He struggled to climb up to the top rope, wobbling like an underprepared tightrope walker.

"A haiku!" he shouted. Everyone turned to look at him. "I'm king of the ring, my reputation is spotless, don't fool with—"

"That's eight," my mom interrupted from below.

"Eight? Huh?"

"That's eight syllables in the second line. A haiku is supposed to have seven."

"It *is* seven," my dad insisted.

"He's right," Mayor Pilkington chimed in from the side of the ring. "Seven."

"Actually, it was eight," Tania Rose said, smoothing out a Band-Aid on the mayor's forehead.

And half of the Lyrical Warriors began muttering to themselves about eights and sevens while counting on their fingers.

I turned back to Mr. Patel. "So . . . do you have any ideas on why he disappeared after that night? Did anything unusual happen?"

Mr. Patel considered, then raised his shoulders. "I remember the image of the Specter in the ring . . . but everything else"—he threw his hands up—"is a distant memory. I was only a little kid, so I wasn't paying much attention to anything other than the wrestlers. If you're looking to solve the mystery of the Specter, I'm afraid I might not be the best witness."

"That's okay," I said, disappointed. I didn't know what I was expecting him to tell me, but I guess I'd wanted something more to work with.

"But . . . ," Arjun started, peering up at the ceiling.

"But what?" I asked. "Do you remember something?"

"Maybe it was my imagination. But I remember the moment the Specter slipped out of the ring and disappeared into the crowd. Like I said, I was enthralled by him. He was my hero. So my eyes were glued to him as he worked his opponent into a stupor. He'd danced around him like a flea on an old dog, and he was just getting ready to perform his final move."

"The Phantom Fling," I said.

"Yes, but he never did it. He was in this corner, right here." Arjun took a step toward the ring and, with some effort, climbed up into it. "He paused and rested against the ropes, like this." Arjun demonstrated the way the Specter had leaned back on the ropes and tilted his head to the ceiling. "Then he scanned the crowd one last time, like he always did before finishing his opponent off. We were all chanting, 'Phantom Fling! Phantom Fling!'

"And I could swear he froze, like this." Arjun stood still, facing out into the audience, his eyes fixed somewhere in the distance. "His whole body went stiff, just for a second. I don't know if anybody else noticed it, but I did. It was just so different from the rest of his movements. He was always like a cat, or like water. But at that moment, he paused. And then he launched back into action. Instead of the Phantom Fling, though, he slid out of the ring. And the rest is history."

"Do you think he saw something in the audience?" I asked. "Or someone, maybe, that made him want to leave?"

Arjun shrugged. "Your guess is as good as mine. I just know what I saw. Say, aren't you kids detectives? Maybe you can figure it out. Now, if you'll excuse me, I've got a spinning dragon kick to perfect."

I sat back down and grabbed a handful of cheese puffs, but I paused before throwing them into my mouth. I kept picturing the Specter in the corner of the ring, looking out into the audience. This place filled with people,

Bellwoodians of another generation, chanting and cheering and having fun. Who else was there that night? Who could the Specter have seen?

The Specter's disappearance was a cold case, unsolved for sixty years. But still, it was fun to think that old Bellwood had had mysteries, too, and now New Bellwood was giving the One and Onlys a fresh case of its own. It was also weird to imagine the rec center, the very room we were in, hosting such a raucous event, with the locals pouring in to witness it. There must have been all kinds of interesting characters in Bellwood back then. I'd have liked to get in a time machine and meet some of the quirky residents, to ask them what they loved—and didn't love—about the town.

Looking around the room, I could see clearly that the Bellwoodians were still a peculiar group of people. Not much had changed there. Mr. Marconi was wandering around the place, trying to locate the foam mustard that had come loose from his enormous bratwurst costume. Mrs. Patel was guessing people's shoe sizes by feeling their feet, with her eyes closed. Dr. Dave was holding a Butter Baby's milkshake up to the light and wondering aloud about its ingredients, while Darrel Sullivan, wearing badger leggings and his Bellwood Pet Store uniform, was munching on a Bozo bar in the ring.

Wait a second . . .

"Bozo bar alert!" I said, nearly spitting out the half

mouthful of cheese puffs I'd been working. I jabbed a finger in the direction of Darrel Sullivan.

"Good find!" Paul said, leaning a little closer and narrowing his eyes on Darrel.

"Darrel Sullivan is always suspicious," Peephole said, ogling him. "Anybody who bleaches their goatee white has something to hide."

That was hard to argue with. And Peephole was right: Darrel Sullivan had always been a little sketchy. We'd crossed paths with him before, and you could count on him hiding at least three things at any given time. Still, even I knew that a Bozo bar was not enough evidence to go after him.

"Bozo bars are delicious," I said, "but he's not the only one who likes them. See?"

I pointed over at Mrs. Patel, who was eating one by the side of the ring. And then at Tania Rose, who was carrying snacks from the vending machine to the mayor. In her hands she had a bag of potato chips, some corn curls, and two Bozo bars.

"True . . . ," Paul began. He had that look in his eye that meant he was onto something. "But we *did* see Darrel at A Pizza Heaven that day, didn't we?"

"Yeah, along with the rest of Bellwood," I said.

"But Darrel was walking across the street, away from A Pizza Heaven. Alone. And he was walking *to* the new place before anybody else was."

"Also true," I said, "but that doesn't mean much."

"No, but it's a couple of facts, and we can't ignore them. And we can't ignore the rats and the hamsters, either, can we?"

"I'd like to," Peephole said.

"Let's think for a minute. If you wanted to get a whole bunch of rats, where would you go?" Paul continued.

"The sewer, maybe?" I answered. "But it would be a lot of work to gather them. Maybe a pet store?"

"And how about hamsters? A *lot* of hamsters."

"Definitely a pet store!" Dorothea said excitedly.

"Darrel works at the Bellwood Pet Store!" Peephole shouted, startling Trillium. She giggled, burped, cried, then spat up on his shoulder.

"Who else would have access to all those rats and hamsters?" Paul asked.

We looked over at Darrel, who was finishing up his Bozo bar and smoothing his hair. He took a big, gloopy bite, and our glances met. He scowled. I scowled back.

"Looks like we're crossing paths one more time with Darrel Sullivan," I said. "Our new prime suspect."

12

The Temperamental Long-Haired Peruvian Guinea Pig

"Maybe he's still holding a grudge against us from what happened in our last investigation," I said, slamming my locker shut. "Remember the X on Paul's parents' bratwurst truck? He could be out to get you."

Paul and Peephole and I were gathering our things at the end of the school day, trying to figure out what possible motive Darrel Sullivan might have for sabotaging Dr. Dave's, A Pizza Heaven, and Honest Bratwurst.

"I guess," Paul said, "but then why not just target the bratwurst truck? No, I've got a feeling it's more complicated than that. Why would he want to push everybody to the new places?"

"Maybe he owns them and stands to make a fortune if everybody in Bellwood eats there," I suggested.

"But he doesn't own them," Peephole said. "He works at the Bellwood Pet Store, remember?"

"I know," I said, bobbing in and out of the crowd of middle schoolers excited about the weekend, "but maybe he works for somebody who does?"

"There's one other thing that doesn't make sense. We know that somebody has been operating the crow from Munchaus's shoe, right? But we saw the crow flying at A Pizza Heaven right after we saw Darrel walking away. He couldn't have been the one flying the crow."

"What if he had the remote hidden? Like, under his shirt?" Peephole asked.

"Or maybe he's got an accomplice. Another person who is in on it," Paul suggested.

"The truth is, we can guess all day long and get nowhere," I said impatiently. "We've got to get in Darrel Sullivan's face about this."

"Usually, I'd say we should take it slow," Paul said as we turned the corner and headed toward the open front doors of Bellwood Middle School. "But I just keep thinking about those X's on the map. We don't have time to wait. Shanks is right. We've got to confront Darrel Sullivan."

"I was afraid you were going to say that," Peephole said. "Does that mean we have to go to the pet store? I don't like pet stores."

"C'mon, Peephole, all the animals are in cages anyway. It's not like they're going to bite you," I said.

"I know, but they can still see me. I get uncomfortable when animals look at me. That's why I don't go to the zoo."

We finally squeezed ourselves through the crowd of kids and teachers and out the big open doors. Everybody had a slightly confused look on their face as they sniffed the air. It hit us immediately, too. Or hit our *noses* immediately.

Worry cast a shadow over Paul's face. "Is that—"

"Maple syrup!" I said. "And it makes me hungry for a Swine in a Sleeping Bag at your parents' bratwurst truck. It's a sweet smell, but it can only mean one thing."

"A pancake factory exploded?" Peephole guessed.

"It means that we're too late to confront Darrel Sullivan at the pet store. My guess is he'll soon be at Honest Bratwurst. Maybe he'll have some rats with him."

"Or hamsters," Peephole said.

"And a robot crow," I added. "Let's hit it!"

We hopped on our bikes and pedaled off as hard as we could. We needed to get over to the bratwurst truck before Darrel Sullivan had a chance to drive the customers away. If we could catch him in the act, with witnesses, this case would be wrapped up. I was beginning to feel confident we might be getting close to cracking it.

Luckily, Honest Bratwurst was a straight shot from the middle school, so we hit the open road and stood up on our bikes for maximum speed.

"There!" Paul yelled, lifting one hand from his handlebars and pointing at a black shape coming up behind us in the sky. It was flying low enough that we could hear the steady whirring as it passed by over our heads.

"The robot crow!" I yelled. "It's going to beat us to the food truck!"

I hunched down over the handlebars and gritted my teeth, pumping my legs as fast as they could go. I pulled away from Paul and Peephole and was the first one to skid into the parking lot of Honest Hardware, where a crowd of people had already gathered at the bratwurst truck. I whipped my head around to look across the street. The Brewster House was still there, but there was a glossy pink-and-blue sign above it that read PIGGY CAKES! Below the words was a cartoon pig, licking his lips over a stack of pancakes. I recognized the name. There was a Piggy Cakes in Schuylerville that my family had been to. Another chain. *So this was the restaurant that was trying to replace Honest Bratwurst,* I thought.

I hopped off the bike and pushed my way through the crowd in search of Darrel Sullivan, but there was no sign of him. Up in the sky, the robot crow was hovering above the truck, its wings flapping in a way that almost made it look real.

"Shanks!" a voice from the crowd called out. I turned to see Dorothea and Elvis running toward me. "I smelled the syrup as soon as I got out of school," Dorothea said. "We came as quickly as we could. The crow is already here!"

"And it's only a matter of time before it sprays its smell," Paul panted, appearing at my side. Peephole popped up next to him, sweating from the furious ride.

"There you are!" Mrs. Marconi yelled from inside the truck, pointing a dripping spatula at us. Her hair was disheveled, and her apron was splattered with pancake batter. "Paul, we could use some help back here. We're swamped!"

"Mom, has anything weird happened yet?" Paul called back.

"I'll say," Paul's dad said, poking his head up from behind the counter. "We've never had so many customers all at once! Must be that maple syrup smell in the air. Now c'mon, Paul, hop back here. Somebody needs to take these orders!"

"But . . . ," Paul began, his eyes darting from the robot crow in the air to the crowd around us.

"No buts! Right now, Paul!"

Paul turned to us with a desperate look.

"Go ahead," I said. "You help your parents. We got this."

Paul sighed and nodded, then ran off to the back of the truck.

"Why hasn't the crow let out its skunk spray yet?" Peephole whispered. "This place is swarming with people."

"In the past, the spray and the rodents have come at the same time," I whispered back. "Any sign of Darrel Sullivan?"

The crowd had a lot of familiar faces: the Beverly twins, Agnes Wiseacre, the Patels, Principal Samuels. Again, it looked like half of Bellwood was arriving.

"I don't see him any—"

"There he is!" Peephole hissed, always with the eagle eye.

Sure enough, Darrel Sullivan was standing on the edge of the crowd, just a few feet away from the line. He was holding what looked like a cloth-draped box. He had an odd expression on his face, too, like he was unsure of himself. His gaze swiveled from the food truck to Piggy Cakes across the street.

I squinted and caught a glimpse of a corner of what Darrel was holding. "He's got a cage!" I said. "He's going to release his creatures any minute!"

But just before we sprang after him, Darrel abruptly turned and walked away from the crowd, the cage still covered. At the same time, the whirring of the robot crow got louder, and we looked up to see it perched right on the roof of the bratwurst truck.

"Let's grab that crow!" Elvis yelled, excited to add another toy to his collection.

"He's right," Dorothea said. "We *should* try to get the crow."

"But we can't let Darrel get away!" I protested. "I'm going after him. Who's coming with me?"

"But . . . but . . . ," Peephole said, clearly not liking either option. I could see that he was calculating which would be worse: tackling a man carrying unknown rodents, or trying to trap a robot bird with skunk powers.

"I'll help you capture the crow," Elvis said, peering up at Peephole.

"You will?" Peephole looked down at him.

"We'll stuff it in here," he said, tugging Dorothea's backpack off her shoulder.

"Be careful." The look on Dorothea's face said she knew this was a bad idea. Still, she turned to me and yelled, "C'mon! Let's go get that guy with the goatee!"

We dashed through the crowd toward Darrel. We'd almost made it all the way to him when he turned and saw us coming. Panic spread across his face, and he broke into a sprint, the cloth slipping off the cage as it swung back and forth with his stride. It was hard to say for sure, but it looked like there was some kind of rodent in there.

"Come back here!" I growled. Not surprisingly, Darrel didn't listen. He led us across the street, toward the Brewster House.

For a guy carrying a cage, Darrel Sullivan was fast. He might have even gotten away if not for the giant talking pig that suddenly emerged from the doorway of Piggy Cakes, carrying a large tray of samples.

"Howdy, folks! It's a piiiiiggyriffic day to taste a Piggy—"

Slammo!

Darrel Sullivan crashed into the pig, knocking its giant head off and sending them both to the ground.

Dorothea and I tried to leap out of the way, but we got tangled up in the heap and fell on top.

"My head!" cried the freckled teenager in the piggy costume. He pawed the ground around him with his big pink hands.

"Hector! Are you okay?!" Darrel Sullivan yelped.

"My name is Lewis," the teenager grunted, "and I'm a little shaken up, but fine."

"Where's Hector?" Darrel Sullivan scrambled to his feet, holding tight to the empty cage. In the collision, it had popped open and the mystery rodent had escaped.

Dorothea and I hopped to our feet, too, twirling like mad and scanning the ground around us for a furball on the loose. Sure enough, out of the corner of my eye, I caught a glimpse of a hairy lump scuttling away. Without thinking, I dived on it, wrestling it into my arms.

"There's no escape now, Darrel! I've got your . . . your . . . uh . . ." I looked down at the thing in my hands, which resembled a loaf of bread with a wig on top of it.

"What *is* that thing?" Dorothea asked.

Darrel reached out and snatched the little creature from me. "Hector is a long-haired Peruvian guinea pig, and he's very temperamental." He stroked the thing gently and whispered to it. "And he doesn't appreciate being yelled at."

"Well, excuse me for frightening your little mop friend, but *I* don't appreciate you trying to scare people away from my friend's bratwurst truck!"

"Whatever you all have going on here, I can't be involved," the teenager in the piggy outfit said, gathering himself to his feet. "I have too many bacon-wrapped wieners to hand out." He popped his head back on and strode into the Brewster House.

"Admit it." I pointed a finger at Darrel Sullivan. "You were going to let that thing loose in front of Paul's bratwurst truck. You wanted people to get scared and run over here to Piggy Cakes. And it was you who brought the hamsters to A Pizza Heaven and the rats to Dr. Dave's."

Darrel shot me a surprised look.

"That's right," I continued, on a roll, "we know all about it. And we know you got them from the pet store you work at."

Darrel cast his eyes down guiltily at Hector, then looked at the crowd in front of Honest Bratwurst across the street.

"And," I kept going, "we know about you snacking on your precious Bozo bars out in Munchaus's shoe, and about the crow and that horrible stench it sprays from its weird robot beak."

His expression turned from surprised to confused. "What's she talking about?" he asked Dorothea.

"You have to admit it," Dorothea said. "We caught you with this . . . this . . ."

"Hector," Darrel said.

"You were going to release it, weren't you?"

He studied us for a moment, then let out a big sigh. "Yeah, okay, I was going to let Hector go. But I didn't! I decided against it! Didn't you see that I was walking away?"

"If you weren't doing anything wrong, then how come you ran from us?" I asked.

"Because you were chasing me!" he said defiantly. "Look, I admit it, okay? I brought Hector here to release him. And"—his eyes darted to the side—"I was responsible for the rats and the hamsters. And yeah, I have a Bozo bar occasionally, but that's between me and my sweet tooth. So what? I don't know anything about a shoe or a . . . robot crow?"

"Oh, no?" I replied. "If you're not responsible for the robot crow, then why are you trying to ruin those restaurants?"

"Whoa." Darrel put a hand up defensively. "I'm not trying to ruin anything." His face softened. "In fact, Honest Bratwurst has the best bratwurst in town. Everybody knows that. But I wasn't born yesterday. I can put the clues together just like you can. It looks like somebody has it out for your friend's place. I just realized that now, and that's why I decided against it." He held Hector up.

"Besides," he added, "Hector and I have gotten to know each other a little, and I wouldn't do that to him."

"I don't get it," Dorothea said, scratching her head. "If you're not the one controlling the crow, and you *don't* have it out for anybody, then why did you release those rats and hamsters?"

Darrel Sullivan shrugged. "Somebody paid me to do it. Actually, they wanted rats for all three places, but I used up the pet store's whole supply on Dr. Dave's. Hamsters were the next best thing, and when we ran out of those, old Hector was the only thing left."

Dorothea and I looked at each other. "Let me guess," I said. "Somebody wrote you a letter with some cash included, promising to pay you more if you took the animals from the pet store and released them at the restaurants?"

Darrel nodded. "Three letters, actually. One for each restaurant. How'd you know that?"

"Call it a hunch," I said.

"You kids must be real detectives," he said, "because I haven't told a soul about any of this."

"Of course we're real detectives," I said. "I thought you'd have figured that out by now. Didn't you think it was odd that somebody was paying you to release rats?"

"At first, I didn't ask any questions," Darrel admitted. "The letter just said to take the rats to a particular address and let them loose. I didn't know it was Dr. Dave's until I got there. I thought it was a little weird, but I decided to just take the money and follow the instructions. And I thought, *Who knows? Maybe Dr. Dave himself is the one who wrote the letter.*"

"Why would Dr. Dave pay you to scatter rats at his restaurant?" I asked. "That doesn't make any sense."

Darrel Sullivan shrugged. "All I'm saying is, people do weird things for publicity. Maybe it was to promote a new flavor, like . . . Rocky Rodent."

"That doesn't sound very good," Dorothea said.

"Hey, don't yuck somebody else's yum. Besides, I needed the money. I'd just wrecked my truck, and I didn't have the money to buy a new one."

"How'd you wreck it? Did you drive into a lake or something?" I asked.

"A Christmas tree, actually. See, I was trying out some modifications I'd made. I put some wings on the side of the truck and was out in a field testing to see if I could lift off with it."

"There's no way that worked," I said.

"It *would* have," Darrel said defensively. "But I lost control of the truck, splashed through a creek, and crashed into a Christmas tree farm."

"Christmas trees? But it's September," Dorothea protested.

"What? You think they pop up fully grown on December first? Anyway, I was in bad need of some cash, and when I got another letter with the promise of even more money, I thought, *What's the harm?* But I saw the same thing happen at A Pizza Heaven: everybody left and went to the new place across the street. And poor old Mrs. Lombardi was left behind. This time"—he nodded his head at Honest Bratwurst—"I just couldn't bring myself to do it."

"So you have no idea who paid you to do this?" I asked.

"None," Darrel Sullivan said. "I'm real good at not asking questions. But now . . . I guess I am starting to get curious."

"Any chance you still have any of the letters?" Dorothea asked.

Darrel bit his lip and stared at us, as if weighing something in his mind. Then he reached into his back pocket and pulled out an envelope. "This arrived under my door yesterday. It's the third one I've gotten."

He handed it to us. I took it and pulled the letter out of the envelope.

"Same thick, cream-colored paper," I observed, "with round corners at the bottom. And same handwriting. Neat cursive, slightly smudged. The paper looks a little shorter than a regular sheet, and . . . what's this?" I pointed to the top of the paper, where there were a few ink marks at the very edge. "Did the person write something up here? Maybe testing the pen out?"

"I don't think so," Dorothea said. "These marks look

like they were printed onto the paper, not written by hand with a pen. And look, the top edge isn't straight across."

"So?" Darrel Sullivan asked.

"So, that means that whoever wrote this letter most likely cut the top of the paper off themselves," Dorothea explained. "And they probably did that because there was something printed up there that gave away their identity."

"Did the other letters have anything printed at the top?" I asked.

Darrel looked up at the sky for a moment, then shook his head. "Nope. I would have noticed that."

The letter gave Darrel instructions to release the rats at the bratwurst truck, with the promise of more cash after it was done.

"They won't be happy you didn't do it this time," Dorothea said.

"Whoever they are." Darrel nodded. "But we don't care, do we, Hector?"

If Hector gave any kind of response, I didn't see it. His hair was too long and silky to see his face.

I suddenly remembered something. I held the letter up to the light. "The watermark! It's on this one, too."

The faint, tiny outline of the crow on the bottom corner of the paper seemed to stare back at us.

Darrel squatted down and opened the cage, gently

placing Hector back inside. "Well, kids, since I haven't really committed any crime, and I'm not the one you're looking for, I'll be on my way." He closed the cage and hoisted it up, Hector peering out through the wire sides. "And next time you decide to investigate a mystery, try not to tackle me again."

"That's up to you," I said. "You keep your nose clean, we won't have to."

Darrel glared down at me, then flicked his head in the direction of Honest Bratwurst. "By the way . . . either your friends are trying to join the circus, or they're having some troubles."

Dorothea and I turned and looked across the street. Elvis was sitting on Peephole's shoulders, and the two of them were staggering this way and that as Peephole tried to keep his balance. He had a look of fierce concentration on his face, using all of his strength to keep them both from toppling to the ground. Elvis, on the other hand, looked like he was loving every second of it. He was grinning from ear to ear when he reached up to drop Dorothea's backpack over the robot crow on the roof of Honest Bratwurst. He quickly clutched the bag to his chest, giggling as the crow inside darted back and forth, seeming to try to escape.

We ran across the street just as Peephole was carefully lowering Elvis back to the ground. Paul jumped out of the back of the food truck and ran to our side.

"Remind me never to do that again," Peephole said exhaustedly.

"We got it!" Elvis declared, opening the bag to show us.

Dorothea and I peeked in, and a pair of red eyes peered up at us.

As a team, we'd managed to capture the robot crow. And this time, we weren't going to let it get away.

13

Let's Get Historical

The garbage truck rumbled up in front of my house, reaching out its mechanical claw to grasp our trash bin. With a rattling jerk, the claw dumped everything into the truck's open back, then pounded the bin onto the sidewalk. It lurched forward and did the same thing to the Hightowers' trash, then the Chens', then the Simons'. One by one, it devoured all the garbage on my block. It was on a mission, and nothing was going to stop it. I felt the same way.

I sat on my front porch, surveying the scene around me. Aside from garbage pickup, Saturday mornings were usually quiet on my street. When the noise of the truck became a distant clattering, I could hear the tweet of birds and the rustle of the early-fall breeze through the trees. That was what my street had always been like, for as long as I could remember. I wondered if it had been like that when my parents were kids in Bellwood. Or Mr. Nemo. Or Dorothea's grandpa.

I peeked into the backpack at my feet. The robot crow was still there, but its eyes were no longer glowing red. In fact, the crow hadn't stirred all night. I kept it in the bag under my bed, checking on it periodically. Maybe somebody turned it off with a remote, or maybe it had run out of battery. Either way, it gave no sign of life. No sudden whirring, no awful stenches.

Around the corner, Paul and Peephole rode into view. I gave them a little wave as they approached.

"Oh, good," Peephole said, braking to a stop. "You survived the night with the crow."

"Pssht," I said, waving my hand in the air. "I wasn't scared for a minute." That wasn't strictly true. I might or might not have slept with my baseball bat next to me in bed. And a clothespin on my dresser to plug my nose. But Peephole didn't need to know that.

"Any weird smells or noises?" Paul asked.

"Aside from my dad when he first wakes up? Nope," I said. "Between us capturing the crow and Darrel Sullivan changing his mind about releasing the . . . the . . ."

"Hector," Peephole said.

"Yeah, *Hector* . . . it seems like we foiled the plan."

"Yeah, but whose plan?" Paul asked. "Whoever it is, they'll probably try again. If they've gone to the trouble of recruiting Mr. Nemo and Darrel Sullivan to do their dirty work, they're probably pretty determined."

"So are we," I said.

"You made it!" a voice called from next door. Dorothea Hightower stood on her front step, smiling broadly at us and waving.

"You think we'd miss a Bellwood Junior Historical Society meeting?" I asked, standing up and crossing the lawn to her house. "Not for the world. Do you expect a lot of people?"

"Yeah," Dorothea said. "You all, me, and Elvis."

"Perfect," Paul said. "That way we can keep discussing the case."

"Go ahead and pop your shoes off, then follow me! The meeting is down in the basement," she said, ushering us through the front door. "We've got snacks. Cheese puffs, chips, chocolate pretzels . . ."

We flipped our shoes off, and Dorothea led us through the living room and down the stairs. Our feet were greeted by fuzzy green carpet, which, combined with the wood-brown paint on the walls and ceiling, gave the basement a foresty vibe. There was a big white bedsheet covering something on the floor, as big as a table but bumpy. Next to it, Dorothea's little brother, Elvis, stared up at us through his thick black glasses.

"Hey, Elvis," I said.

Elvis saluted. "I'm getting a T. rex today."

At this point, I was used to Elvis saying weird things. "Oh, yeah? Where are you going to keep it?"

"In my toy bin," he said. "It's a remote-controlled T. rex with realistic roaring sounds and crush-o-matic jaws. It takes a whole pack of batteries to run."

"Sounds awesome," Paul said.

"Sounds kind of scary," Peephole muttered.

"Did you bring the crow?" Elvis asked.

I handed him the backpack, which he eagerly opened. He pulled the crow out and grinned.

"I'm going to have the crow and T. rex fight. It's going to be epic," he said, then started flying it around the room, for some reason making jet noises. Suddenly, he stopped and said, "Or maybe they won't fight. Maybe they'll be the greatest of friends."

"We can hope," I said.

We took seats on the floor around the bedsheet while Dorothea offered us a bag of cheese puffs. On the walls were newspaper clippings from the *Bellwood Noise*, our local newspaper. "Highway Rerouted, Bellwood Falls on Tough Times," one faded gray headline read. "Mayor Munchaus's Bratwurst Bonanza a Big Success!" was another. "Wildfires Threaten Bellwood," a more recent newspaper warned. And finally, a front page from just a month ago: "Town Eyes Future with New Bellwood Project."

"You really like history, huh?" Paul said, gazing at the clippings.

Dorothea looked at the walls proudly. "I believe that you have to understand where you're coming from to know where you want to go, if you get what I mean. If we don't appreciate our past, we can't know what kind of future we want. Don't you agree?"

"Absolutely," Peephole said through a mouthful of cheese puffs. "And did you mention pretzels?"

Elvis flew the crow over to a snack bin in the corner, grabbed a bag of pretzels, and flipped them to Peephole, who was surprised by the projectile but still managed to catch it before it hit him in the face.

"You could look up old newspaper articles, too, if you wanted," Dorothea said. "You can search the archive on the Bellwood Library website. Sometimes when I'm bored, I'll just pick a random date from the past and read the whole newspaper. Come to think of it, it is sort of like stepping into a time machine."

"When I'm bored, I pick my belly button lint with tweezers," Elvis said.

I nodded, and Peephole looked personally offended.

"Anyway, your knowledge of our past has sure come in handy so far on this case," I said.

Dorothea smiled, then cleared her throat. "Let's get started! I thought I'd begin today's meeting by showing you all a project I've been working on for quite some time." She reached down, grabbed hold of the bedsheet, and carefully raised it to reveal the entire town of Bell-wood. Miniature Bellwood, that is.

"Wow," I said. It was all there. The grid of streets, the tiny houses, the little green trees lining our blocks. It was Bellwood, the town we all knew so well, but shrunk into a tabletop version.

"It's taken me months of work," Dorothea said, proudly witnessing our reactions. "I wanted to create a scale model of Bellwood exactly the way it was this past summer, *before* the New Bellwood project began. I had a feeling the town would look pretty different in a matter of years, so this was a chance for me to offer a snapshot of the old Bellwood."

"It's like a tiny movie set," Paul marveled.

The details were incredible. I leaned in closer to see the little buildings and homes and restaurants and cars frozen in time. There, in the southwest corner of town, was the empty drive-in movie field that now housed the Conquistador. And there was my house in the northwest corner, with Dorothea's right next to it. And blanketing the outer edge of the tiny bell-shaped town were the trees that made up the Bell Woods.

"This is amazing," Paul said. "There's Honest Hardware!" He pointed to a small building in the center of town.

"And here's my house!" Peephole laughed.

"And here's my house!" I pointed.

"There's my shoe," Elvis said, looking at a silver sneaker up in the far northeast corner of the mini-Bellwood. "I've been looking for that!" He reached out to grab it, but Dorothea swiped at his hand.

"Wait!" she said. "I actually need that there until I can craft a proper replacement for it. It's a little too big to actually be to scale, but it's close enough."

"Let me guess: Munchaus's giant shoe statue?" Paul asked.

"One and the same." Dorothea smiled.

The sound of the front doorbell rang out and Elvis sprang to his feet. "T. rex!" he shouted, then zipped up the stairs.

"Here's your parents' bratwurst truck," Dorothea said, pointing to a little vehicle in the center of town. "And here's the Brewster House. Or, I guess, Piggy Cakes."

A sad look came over Dorothea's face. I remembered her crusade to turn the Brewster House into a museum. I felt awful. We had told her we were going to help, but we'd forgotten all about it in the midst of our own investigation.

"It should be a museum," I said. "Bellwood doesn't need a Piggy Cakes. It needs to understand its past. We're a great town. But we're not perfect. And that's important to learn about. There's got to be a way to convince Mayor Pilkington to save it."

"Thanks," Dorothea said, casting her eyes down at her model's tiny Brewster House. "But it's not really up to him. The town council made the decision. In fact, Mayor Pilkington seemed really impressed when I handed him all those signatures."

"How can we convince the town council, then?" I asked. I wasn't ready to give up just yet.

Dorothea shrugged and gazed down at Bellwood. Or, Bellwood the way it used to be.

An electronic roar startled us. Elvis was standing at the bottom of the stairs, holding up his new T. rex. There was an envelope stuck in its crush-o-matic jaws.

"What's that?" Dorothea asked.

"A letter that came in the mail. It's for you."

Dorothea hopped up and crossed over to Elvis, carefully retrieving the letter from the T. rex's teeth. She tore it open and read it aloud.

From the Desk of Mayor Frank Pilkington

Dear Ms. Hightower,

    First, let me tell you how inspired I am by your drive and your vision. As you know, Bellwood has a long and storied history of innovative citizens creating positive change in our community, and I can tell that you have that same passion. As your mayor, I'd like to commend your interest in our town's past, and let you know that even though the Brewster House is currently being used as a restaurant, I believe that a Bellwood History Museum is a necessary and important initiative, and I'd like to offer my help. . . .

And that's when I stopped listening, because I recognized the paper that she was reading from. Paul and Peephole recognized it, too. They both stood straight up.

"Let me see that!" I yelped, scrambling to my feet and running across the basement to Dorothea.

"Oh, uh, sure—"

"Thanks," I said, snatching it from her hands.

The paper was thick and cream-colored, with rounded bottom corners, just like the letters that Mr. Nemo and Darrel Sullivan had received. The only differences were that this letter was full-sized, the message typed instead of written by hand, and the top corners of the paper were rounded, too. At the top of the page, printed in thick brown letters, were the words FROM THE DESK OF MAYOR FRANK PILKINGTON. Down at the bottom, though, handwritten in big, clear letters, was the signature:

Your Mayor, Frank Pilkington

"The watermark! Is it the same?" Paul said.

I held the paper up to the fluorescent ceiling light. There it was: the little crow.

I lowered the letter and nodded slowly at Paul. He stared back, his jaw hanging down.

"Whoa," he said.

"Of *course!*" I said, snapping my fingers. "Pilkington works at Town Hall, which is right across the street from Munchaus Park. He probably saw Mr. Nemo drop off the crows from his office window! He could have run over, snatched them, and bolted back to his office before Mr. Nemo was out of the restroom!"

"And we saw him eating Bozo bars at the Lyrical Warriors meeting the other night," Paul added.

"I *knew* it was somebody important," Peephole said.

"Doesn't get more important than the mayor," I said.

"My mom is more important," Elvis said.

"So Mayor Pilkington is mixed up with the robot crow after all?" Dorothea asked.

Paul sighed. "Looks like it."

"We have to get him!" I cried, heading for the basement stairs.

"He's the mayor!" Peephole said. "We can't just 'get him.'"

I turned to him. "We can't *not* get him! He's the one!" I held up Dorothea's letter as proof. "What more evidence do we need?"

"We *do* need to confront him," Paul said.

"Finally, somebody is making sense." I turned back to the stairs.

"But not yet," Paul continued. "Peephole's right. Mayor Pilkington may seem kind of bumbling, but he is powerful. We have to be careful who we tell about this. If we confront him alone, he'll just deny it. We need to do it with witnesses, put him on the spot."

"We need evidence," Dorothea said. "More than just

the letter. We need something that shows Mayor Pilkington is behind all this."

We stood still, staring at Dorothea's miniature Bellwood and waiting for an answer.

Dorothea snapped her fingers. "The shoe! We know that Pilkington has been at Munchaus's shoe. Maybe there's some evidence up there that we can use."

"It's worth a try," Paul said. "Let's go for a ride!"

We rushed up the stairs, out of the house, and onto our bikes. If Pilkington was behind all this, we were going to stop him, and nothing was going to get in our way.

"It's empty," Dorothea said, standing in the doorway of Munchaus's giant shoe. We'd hustled up to the northeast corner of the Bell Woods as quickly as we could, but we weren't expecting to find this.

"I don't understand . . . it was all here!" I said in disbelief. "The map, the chair, the table . . ."

"The Bozo bar wrapper," Peephole said.

"He cleared it out," Paul said, shaking his head. "He must have known we were here. But how?"

"Maybe he saw those," Dorothea said, pointing down at the floor. There were footprints of dried dirt all over. They were definitely from the last time we were here.

"Whoops," Peephole said. "Now what?"

"Now," I said, "we call out Pilkington anyway! I'm tired of waiting around."

"But it's going to be our word against his, remember?" Peephole sighed. "He's the mayor, and we're just a few kids with a weird story about a stinky robot crow and some hamsters. We have no evidence!"

"We *do* have evidence," I said. "Remember? We have one of the crows."

"I guess you can borrow it," Elvis said.

"So . . . when do we confront him?" Dorothea asked.

Paul grinned. "Where do we know Pilkington will be on Monday night? Along with a big group of people?"

"Lyrical Warriors Poetry Wrestling Club," Peephole answered. "So . . . what's the plan?"

We looked at each other in silence, waiting for an idea.

"Did anybody bring snacks?" Peephole asked.

Dorothea grinned and pulled the bag of pretzels from her sweatshirt. "I always come prepared."

The five of us sat on the cold cement floor of Munchaus's shoe, crunching pretzels and thinking. Crunching and thinking. Crunching and thinking . . .

And then an idea came and perched in my head.

⟫ 14 ⟪

Nevermore!

Peephole stood outside of the wrestling ring, peering up at the momentarily empty mat. Even through his thick goggles, I could see his look of concern. He'd stuffed two pillows under his extra-large T-shirt—one padding his front, the other his back—and on his hands he wore neon-green rubber gloves.

"You look like a science lab and a mattress store had a baby," I said, poking him in the front pillow.

"Wrestling is an incredibly dangerous activity," he said. "Just in case Pilkington tries to body-slam me, I'll be ready."

"And you'll be ready if he wants to take a nap, too," I said. "But he's not going to body-slam you, I promise."

"How do you know?"

"Because if he tries it, I'll slap a reverse chicken-wing hold on him."

"You qualified to do that hold?" Peephole asked.

"I'm qualified to try to save Bellwood from a power-hungry mayor, if that's what you're asking."

"We agreed on no tackling, remember?" Paul said. "Let's stick to the plan—after all, you came up with it. We get Pilkington up in the ring. We get all eyes and ears on us. And then we recite the poem. Dorothea and Elvis are stationed in the audience near the exit, just in case Pilkington tries to escape."

Dorothea and Elvis nodded their heads, and Elvis cracked his knuckles. "If he comes toward us, I'll activate my superstrength and lift him over my head," Elvis said.

"Yeah," Paul said. "Or maybe just slow him down until the rest of us can catch up. It's a good plan, and it might just work."

"We'll see," I said. Yes, it had been my idea to put him on the spot and confront him with the crow. And yes, I'd stayed up half the night writing a poem to recite—and I wouldn't even be getting school credit for it. But I was still itching for a little more action.

For everyone else there, it was just another Monday-evening Lyrical Warriors session. But for us, this was the night that we were going to expose Mayor Pilkington as crooked. He was manipulating his citizens' minds and tummies, driving them away from their old favorites and toward his idea of New Bellwood. He was trying to mold the future of Bellwood into what he wanted, not what was best for the town.

"Did you bring the crow?" Paul asked.

I nodded and patted the bag slung over my shoulder. When the time was right, this little baby would take center stage. But not quite yet.

It was nearing the end of a water break, five minutes set aside for the members of the Lyrical Warriors to catch their breath, guzzle liquids, argue with the vending machine to hold up its end of the bargain, and chat casually, as if they hadn't just had their faces jammed into each other's armpits.

"There he is." Paul pointed at Mayor Pilkington, who was panting heavily and wiping his face with a towel. He seemed to be dictating some kind of speech to Tania Rose, who was readying a fresh towel with her right hand and scribbling furiously with her left. Behind them, Darrel Sullivan was showing Dr. Dave, the ice cream guy, something on his back, and Dr. Dave kept reminding him that he wasn't a real doctor.

We scooted a little closer to Pilkington, trying to catch what he was saying.

". . . and I make a solemn promise that though we haven't found any evidence of a sewer leak, we'll get to the bottom of these . . . these . . . disgusting . . ."

"'Unpleasant,'" Tania Rose said.

". . . these *unpleasant* aromas as quickly as we can. And in better news, I'm excited to begin phase two of the New Bellwood project, which will feature new stores, new public facilities, new sidewalks—"

"And new robot crows, too," Paul whispered.

"Not if we can help it," I whispered back.

". . . and I know that you'll be excited, too, when—"

"You used 'excited' already," Tania Rose said. "How about 'thrilled'?"

Mayor Pilkington nodded, and droplets of sweat flew from his face. "You'll be *thrilled* to step into the future with me, and soon you'll be as thrilled as I am—"

"'Ecstatic,'" Tania Rose said.

". . . as *ecstatic* as I am about—"

"Sorry to interrupt your speech," Darrel Sullivan said, tapping Mayor Pilkington on the shoulder from behind.

Startled, the mayor whipped his head around and splashed Darrel with a drop or two of sweat. He murmured an apology and dabbed at the younger man's goatee.

"You're the mayor, so you must have some kind of medical training, right?"

"Well, uh, actually—"

"Be honest," Darrel continued, "does this rash look like the state of Ohio to you?"

"Oh, I'm not qualified to . . . Well . . ." The mayor tilted his head. "Looks more like Oklahoma, I'd say."

"Oklahoma?!" Darrel said, twisting around to see his own back.

Tania Rose sighed and shook her writing hand out. She looked tired, and it struck me that it must have been hard to be Pilkington's assistant. He was always moving, always giving speeches, always goofing up. She brushed a tangle of hair out of her face with an ink-stained hand, then glanced over at Darrel Sullivan's back. "It's Arkansas, if anything," she said. "Now, Mayor, you were in the middle of your speech—"

But the bell rang, signaling the end of the break. Pilkington mopped his forehead with the towel, shrugged, and told Tania that he'd finish the speech during the next water break. He began walking down to the ring.

"Excuse me, Mr. Mayor?" I said, jumping in front of him.

"Oh, hello there. Shanks, right?" He smiled at me, and I nodded, shaking his extended hand. "What can I do for you?"

"Well, my friends and I think we're ready to hop into the ring and share some of our poetry, but we're a little nervous."

"I understand," the mayor said. "I'm more of a grappler than a poet myself, but you just have to believe in yourselves."

"Thanks, that means a lot," I said. "Say, do you think you could join us in the ring? We could use your help up there."

Pilkington winked. "You betcha, Shanks. The mayor's number one priority is his citizens."

The mayor climbed into the ring first, followed by Paul and me. Peephole paused at the edge, looking uncertain.

"I don't think I can do this," he muttered. "Maybe I should stay out in the audience with Dorothea and Elvis."

I'd seen this face on him before. He was scared, and he didn't believe in himself. But I knew he *could* do it. Sometimes, a gentle boost of his confidence did the trick.

"Peephole . . . Dorothea and Elvis will be fine by themselves. Now . . . get in the ring or I'm going to put *you* in a chicken-wing hold," I snarled. Other times, you just had to be firm with him.

Peephole reluctantly scrambled into the ring, and the three of us stood and surveyed the crowd. There were all our parents, and Mrs. Newsome, and the manager of the Conquistador, and Mr. Nemo in the back, and all the other wrestler-poets getting ready to enter the ring again. Dorothea and Elvis made their way through the crowd, coming to a stop in front of the exit doors. They turned and gave us the thumbs-up.

"Ladies and gentlemen!" I called out in my best announcer voice. "Are you ready to ruuuuuumble?"

I waited for a thunderous response, but the only reply was Peephole's mom asking, "Is that my pillow?"

"I said, ARE YOU READY TO RUMBLE?!"

This time, Mayor Pilkington whooped and clapped enthusiastically.

"That's good enough," Peephole whispered. "Let's get to it."

"We'd like to introduce ourselves!" I continued. "The most dangerous triple tag team in town, we are . . . uh . . ." I turned to Paul and Peephole and whispered, "We forgot to come up with a wrestling name!"

"We are the Guardians of Bellwood!" Paul shouted. He showed his muscles and stomped on the mat. I growled at the crowd. Peephole made a noise that sounded like he had a stomachache.

"We'd like to recite a poem for you tonight," I said.

There was a spattering of applause from the onlookers, along with some smiles and at least one scowl (Darrel Sullivan was clearly still annoyed with us).

"And we have a special guest with us. Please give it up for our very own Mayor Pilkington!"

The crowd responded with a medium-sized ovation, mixed with a few *woo-hoo*s and hollers. I escorted the mayor to the opposite corner and asked him to stay put.

"This is a poem we call 'The Crow,'" I announced, then cleared my throat.

"Remember," Peephole whispered. "Don't mention the rats."

"I won't," I whispered back. "I don't want you to get nauseous just as we're going to nail him."

Finally, I launched into the poem:

Once upon a Bellwood morning, the town woke up
  to a fragrant warning:
An ice cream scent that made us crave those famous
  scoops from Dr. Dave's—
But as we waited patiently for rocky road or
  mint praline,

Above our heads we heard a humming, and coming
*   from a robot crow,*
The foulest stench we ever sniffed made all the
*   famished people flow*
To Butter Baby's across the road.

"Ah, inspired by 'The Raven,' by Edgar Allan Poe," Mrs. Newsome said appreciatively from the first row. "Very, very nice."

"Now?" Peephole whispered.

"Now!"

Peephole reached into my backpack and pulled out the captured robot crow. He perched it on the corner post opposite Mayor Pilkington.

A tinkling of curious noises rose from the audience. I stared hard at Pilkington. His eyes widened a little at the sight of the crow, and he smiled, as if he was enjoying the show, too. If I thought the unexpected appearance of the crow would make him confess, I was wrong. I launched back into the poem.

With glowing eyes and open beak, the crow let out
*   its awful reek,*
And suddenly we all took flight from Heaven to
*   Slice of Life.*
So one by one we turn our back on all the memories
*   of our past,*

And chew and chomp and smack our lips and
  swallow ourselves in every bite;
And even if it isn't right, Bellwood's future looks so
  bright.
But we won't go without a fight.

"Shanks," my dad whispered. "The poem's supposed to be about a *raven*, remember? Cool prop, though!"

"This is a weird poem," I heard Darrel Sullivan say out in the audience. "But then I never really understood poetry."

A confused murmur spread through the spectators, but Mayor Pilkington smiled at us and winked. "You're doing great," he whispered to me. "Did you write this yourself? It's fantastic! A little odd, though."

I nodded, caught between being proud that the mayor liked my poem and being frustrated that he didn't seem affected by it. The poem was supposed to make him feel so guilty that he would confess. At least squirm a little bit. He was certainly sweating, but not from discomfort. He just stood there, grinning.

"Go on!" he urged.

I looked over to Paul and Peephole. They nodded their encouragement.

But if you think this is a hoax, or merely
  strange coincidence,

There's someone pulling all the strings, a
   mastermind behind closed doors,
Fooling all Bellwoodians: we unsuspecting
   citizens
Can't see what tomorrow brings or what the villain
   has in store.
Will Bellwood ever be the same, like in the good old
   days before?
Quoth the mayor, "Nevermore!"

On the last line, I stepped forward and pointed an accusing finger right into Pilkington's face.

He leaned back a little. The smile stayed on his face, but it wavered, as if I'd just told a joke that he didn't quite get.

There was silence from the audience as I stood there, frozen, with my finger inches from the mayor's nose. Somebody, maybe my dad, clapped once or twice, and then a few more people joined in to produce a little lackluster applause. Somebody sneezed loudly at the door to the restroom. Everybody turned to look at Mr. Patel, who was walking down the aisle with a streamer of toilet paper stuck to his orange boots. Elvis let loose a giggle, and Dorothea shrugged at us with a beats-me look.

This was not what I'd had in mind when I came up with this plan. Pilkington was stonewalling us. And since we didn't have an official plan B, I readied myself for a spinning dragon kick.

"I think I know what's going on here," Pilkington said, flashing the room a friendly smile before turning to us with an open, patient expression.

"You do?" Peephole said, surprised.

"You're not pleased with me, are you? About the restaurants?"

"No," I said quietly, a little stunned. "I mean, no! We're not pleased with you! We know what's been going on! You're trying to ruin Bellwood, one business at a time!"

A few gasps escaped the audience, and Pilkington looked hurt by the accusation. "Ruin Bellwood?" he said, innocently putting a hand to his chest. "I mean, I'll admit that the tomato sauce at Slice of Life is a little too salty, and you can't eat too many Piggy Cakes without getting a tummy ache, but I think you're overreacting."

"He's playing innocent," Paul whispered. "He's not cracking."

"Tummy ache?" I shot back, getting riled up. "No! We're talking about what you're doing to the old restaurants. Dr. Dave's . . . A Pizza Heaven . . . Honest Bratwurst!"

"I know, I know," Pilkington said, putting a hand up to stop me. "I get it, believe me. Change can be hard to get used to. But everything changes eventually. And just because there are new flavors in Bellwood doesn't mean we can't still love our old favorites, right?" He nodded at the audience. "But I, for one, happen to think our New Bellwood eateries are some of the finest in town. Though I can't take credit for them, really. Tania, my assistant, was in charge of that whole aspect of the project, weren't you, Tania?" He glanced to the back of the room. "She's even been personally helping to get Butter Baby's up and running smoothly. Tania, you've done a great job, by the way, and sorry about the tomato sauce comment . . . just one man's opinion. Tania, you here?" Mayor Pilkington put a hand over his eyes to block the light and scanned the audience.

I turned to Paul and Peephole. Their faces were as confused and helpless as mine must have been. "The plan's not working," Peephole whispered as we huddled up. "He's not confessing to anything. Shanks, I never thought I'd say this, but I think you should tackle him."

"Wait!" Paul said, his face taut with concentration. He was trying to work something out in his head.

I was, too. Something that Pilkington said had snagged in my mind. Tania Rose oversaw the restaurants? Not the mayor? But what did that mean? Sometimes, my unconscious brain caught on to clues before the rest of me did.

A question popped into my mind, and I whispered it to Paul and Peephole. "Is Pilkington right-handed or left-handed?"

We all looked at him. He was peering back forlornly as if seeking forgiveness for something. Maybe the tomato sauce.

"Never noticed," Paul said. "Why?"

"I'm thinking about something . . . ," I said. "Peephole, you have a photographic memory. Do you know if he's a righty or a lefty?"

Peephole clearly didn't know why I was asking, but he closed his eyes anyway. His face went blank like it always did when he accessed his photographic memory. After a few seconds, he opened his eyes.

"Righty."

"How do you know?"

"Because when he threw the T-shirt that hit me in the face back at the school assembly, he did it with his right hand."

"Maybe the mayor's innocent act wasn't an act at all," I said.

"What are you thinking about?" Paul asked.

"Left-handed problems," I muttered.

"Huh?" Peephole asked.

Whipping around to the uncertain faces outside of the ring, I bowed ceremoniously and lifted my head high with a big, fake smile. "Thanks for listening to our silly poem!" I turned to Mayor Pilkington and began clapping. "Let's hear it for our guest, the mayor! Thanks for being a good sport during our joke!"

"Joke?" Peephole hissed under his breath. "What are you talking about?"

I escorted the mayor out of the ring to the sound of another weak spattering of confused applause. "Sorry if the poem was a little confusing, Mayor Pilkington," I said. "Let us buy you a Bozo bar to make it up to you."

"No need." Pilkington smiled, raising his hand. "And I'm allergic to nuts, so no Bozo bar for me, thank you. I *could* go for a milkshake, but that's for another time."

"Allergic to Bozo bars?" Peephole gasped as we slunk away from the ring. "But he's lying! We saw him eating Bozo bars the other day!"

"We didn't," Paul said slowly. "We saw Tania carrying Bozo bars, and we assumed they were for the mayor."

"They must have been for her," I said.

"For who?" Dorothea asked, appearing at our side with Elvis.

"Dorothea! There's no way you have the petition with you, is there?" I asked. "The one with all the signatures about turning the Brewster House into a museum?"

Dorothea frowned. "No, sorry. Why do you need it?"

I snapped my fingers in frustration. "Because I have a hunch about something. Do you happen to remember if there were any signatures that were—"

"Smudged," Paul broke in, looking at me and nodding his head. "And written in cursive, too?"

"Ooooh," Peephole whispered. "You're trying to find

a match for the handwriting from the letters to Darrel Sullivan and Mr. Nemo, aren't you?"

"And from the robot crow itself," I whispered back. "And I have a pretty good idea whose writing it might be."

Dorothea bit her lip, trying to remember. "Well, the whole first page was a little smeared because Elvis spilled apple juice on it."

"Did not!" Elvis protested. "It was orange juice."

"What about any smudged names that weren't spilled on?" I asked impatiently.

"I . . . I can't remember," Dorothea answered.

"Maybe I can," Peephole said. We all turned to look at him, surprised. "I flipped through the pages of the petition right before I signed it." He closed his eyes. His face went blank. We waited.

"*Tania Rose,*" he finally said. "On the last page, a few signatures up from where we signed. Her writing was in cursive. And smudged."

I smiled. "That's exactly what I thought. Good work, Peephole!"

"How'd you know?" Peephole asked.

"Earlier tonight," I began, "I noticed Tania Rose had ink stains on her left hand—the same hand she was writing with. It's a common problem for left-handed people, as I know thanks to Mitzi Peters in math class. When they write, the side of their hand smears the wet ink."

"Which explains why all the notes were smudged,"

Paul said. "And so that means that it wasn't Pilkington who was watching from Town Hall when Mr. Nemo dropped off the robot crows in Munchaus Park—"

"It was Tania!" I said. "And that's why the letters were written on Pilkington's stationery, because she probably took the paper from his desk!"

"Whoa," Peephole said. "So now that we know Tania is our suspect, what do we do?"

"We tackle—er, confront her about it! Where is she?"

We swung our heads around, trying to find Tania. She wasn't next to Mayor Pilkington as usual, or over by the vending machine. She wasn't anywhere to be found.

15

An Awfully Dangerous Beverage

"Tania left," Elvis said plainly.

"Huh?" I said.

"It's true." Dorothea nodded. "Halfway through your poem, she ran to the exit. She said she'd forgotten something at Town Hall and had to go get it."

"And you let her go?" I asked.

"Of course," Dorothea said. "Pilkington was our suspect. At least, we thought he was. We didn't know *she* was the one behind it all."

"We've got to find Tania before she can hide the evidence!" I said. "There were two crows! Maybe her new control room is in Town Hall!"

We all sprang for the exit.

"Wait!" Dorothea yelled. "Something's not right. Tania said she was going to Town Hall, but she hopped in the golf cart and went that way." Dorothea pointed west, down the road. "Town Hall is south of here. She should have headed *that* way."

"You're right!" Paul said. "She must have been lying. So her new control station is west, down that way!"

"Yeah," Peephole said. "But . . . where exactly?"

We stopped and looked at each other. He was right. Tania had moved her control room out of Munchaus's giant shoe, and now we had no idea where she was operating from.

"We can figure this out," I said boldly. "I'm just not sure how."

"We need to think logically," Paul said, closing his eyes to concentrate. "We can use reason to make a good guess. What do we know about Tania?"

"Aside from the fact that she's trying to sabotage old Bellwood? Not much," I said. "She's a snappy dresser?"

"Hmm," Paul said, "let's try something else. Where would *you* hide a robot crow control room?"

The five of us sighed impatiently, flitting our eyes around for some kind of an answer. Up in the ring, people were starting to join Mayor Pilkington. Mr. Patel, in his orange jumpsuit, was practicing a limerick, tapping out the rhythm on the ropes. My dad, in his perfect Specter outfit, kept at it with the Phantom Fling: three side steps, a swoop, and then a . . . stumble to the floor.

That reminded me of something my dad said a while back. We'd been talking about what happened to the real Specter and . . . What had he said? Sometimes the best hiding place is right in plain sight?

That's exactly what Tania must have been thinking when she came up with the robot crow idea. They flew right over our heads, and nobody noticed. *Almost* nobody. Would she try something similar with her second control room?

Suddenly, an idea hit me. "What's the most obvious thing in Bellwood?"

"Huh?" Peephole asked. Paul stared blankly at me, too.

"What's the one thing right in the middle of town that you can't miss?"

Peephole shook his head. "You got me."

"The milkshake," Paul said slowly. "The huge Butter Baby's milkshake statue! You think that's where Tania is?"

"Remember what she said to Darrel Sullivan? There's nothing inside of it. She's *been* inside that milkshake. I'll bet anything that's where she is right now!"

"It's a long shot," Paul said, "but it's all we've got."

"Oh, man," Peephole moaned. "That thing creeps me out!"

I was already heading for the door. I whipped around and yelled, "Paul, Peephole, you follow me. Dorothea and Elvis, go tell Mayor Pilkington to meet us at Butter

Baby's in ten minutes! He needs to catch her with the crow!"

"How are they going to get him to go?" Peephole asked.

"We'll tell him his citizens need his help," Dorothea said. "Hurry, Shanks!"

I turned and bolted out the door. Throwing a glance over my shoulder, I saw Paul and Peephole running out of the rec center and mounting their bikes, too. To get to Butter Baby's, all we had to do was blast straight down the street.

Never before had my legs pumped so hard. I stood up and leaned forward into the wind, gritting my teeth. If ever there was a time I needed to ride fast, this was it. Maybe, if I could get into Butter Baby's, there would be a door to a stairwell or a ladder leading up into the giant milkshake. And then, from there, maybe the control room would be open, and maybe I'd be able to catch Tania there with the other crow. That was a lot of maybes.

Up ahead, I caught a glimpse of the giant milkshake on top of Butter Baby's. *I better be right about this*, I said to myself, *because if I'm not, then Tania is somewhere else in Bellwood, clearing away all the evidence of the robot crows. And without evidence, our theory is just a crazy story.* I pumped my legs even harder. Then something in the parking lot of Butter Baby's grabbed my attention. Was it a car? No . . . it was a golf cart! The same lime-green golf cart that Tania drove Mayor Pilkington around in!

As soon as I reached the parking lot, I jumped off my bike and tugged at the front door, which rattled but didn't open.

"She locked the place!" I growled in frustration. "How am I supposed to get into the control room now?" Stepping back from the door, I gaped up at the big milkshake. It was still spinning slowly around, looming high above, mocking me.

I had to think fast. Maybe I could throw a rock through the door and break in that way? But even if I could do it, there'd probably be another locked door on the inside.

And then I remembered what she had told Darrel Sullivan. There was a trapdoor on the top of the milkshake. If I could get up there, I could drop down into the cup.

Paul and Peephole skidded up next to me on their bikes.

"The doors are locked," I said, studying the building. The bike rack was located directly below an overhang, which sloped steeply up toward the flat roof, where the enormous milkshake spun. Splotches of plaster milkshake stuck out from the side of the cup. "The only option is to climb."

"Climb up there?" Peephole said, jabbing a finger at the rotating Butter Baby's. "Are you crazy?"

"It *does* seem awfully dangerous," Paul agreed.

But I knew what I had to do. Reach, grab, pull, scamper. The bike rack provided me with a nice launching pad, and I jumped up and grabbed the edge of the roof with both hands, pulling myself up. Once I was standing on the roof, I clambered toward the milkshake, which looked even bigger up close than it did from the ground. It twisted slowly above me with a mechanical groan.

Drawing a big breath, I tried to plan a climbing route. But my heart sank when I realized that it was impossible. The cup angled up and out, making gravity my enemy, and the splotches of plaster milkshake looked too smooth to grab hold of. I was *sure* that Tania's control room was inside, but how was I supposed to get there?

As the milkshake slowly turned, the answer was revealed. A ladder, camouflaged in the same red and white as the giant cup, jutted out from its side.

I leapt with everything I had, grabbing the bottom rung of the ladder when it swung directly above me. My feet scraped the bottom of the cup as I secured my footing.

And then I broke the golden rule of climbing. I looked down. Below me in the parking lot, Paul and Peephole seemed impossibly far away. My face flushed with heat and my throat felt tight. Suddenly, my breath stopped in my chest. In my head, I heard only the loud *whoosh* of nothingness.

I'd climbed much higher than this before, so what

was the problem? My vision blurred. A thought invaded my mind: *Just like Funston's Oak. Only this time, you'll fall.* I tried to push the thought away, but my mind wouldn't cooperate.

"You okay, Shanks?" Paul called up.

I couldn't respond.

Peephole looked up, too, and immediately recognized the panic on my face.

"Just breathe," he urged. "Shanks, tell me three things you see."

I breathed and closed my eyes for a couple of seconds. When I opened them, I was looking at the twirling milkshake. "I see a giant milkshake."

"Good!" Peephole said calmly. "Now two more things."

Swallowing, I tilted my head even farther back. "The sky. It's pink. The sun is setting." I looked down at Peephole and Paul. "And I see you two. My best friends."

"That's right," Peephole said in a steady voice. "Shanks, you can do this. You're the bravest person I know."

"But I'm scared." I shook my head. I'd said a lot of weird things in my life, but that simple sentence felt the strangest coming out of my mouth. And yet it was true. There was no denying it now.

"Of course you are," Peephole said. "You're hanging on to a spinning milkshake fifty feet up in the air. But being brave is not about being fearless. It's about facing the fears you have."

I nodded down to him, then turned my attention back to the top of the milkshake. *One leg, then the other,* I said to myself. With every step, I felt braver and braver. At the top of the ladder, I reached up to grip the lid of the milkshake.

Fwip!

My foot slipped free from the ladder. My chest lurched, and I let out a tiny whimper as the earth tried to pull me back to it. With one hand, I hung on with everything I had, my legs dangling.

But my body knew what to do. My other hand shot up and gripped the lid, and with a mighty grunt, I heaved myself up onto the milkshake.

"Woo-hoo!" Paul yelled, ecstatic.

"Now don't fall in!" Peephole shouted up.

To my relief, I immediately noticed a handle poking up from the lid of the milkshake. I gripped it with both hands and wrenched it upward. The door swung open more easily than I'd guessed it would, almost making me stumble over the edge. But I regained my balance and peered down through the opening, the evening sun shining over my shoulder into the cavernous cup.

"Freeze!" I shouted, which was kind of a funny thing to say into a giant milkshake.

A face swiveled up to look at me. And though the eyes that locked with mine were squinting into the light, I could tell they were both surprised and guilty. Another pair of eyes gleamed—the glowing red eyes of the robot crow curled in Tania Rose's arm. In her left hand, the mayor's assistant held a flashlight.

We stared at each other for a long second. "We got you," I said, my voice echoing off the round walls of the dark room.

In a level, steady voice, she replied, "Not yet."

She clicked the flashlight off, and once again, Tania vanished into the shadows.

⇒ 16 ⇐

Breaking Kayfabe

"She's on the run!" I shouted to Paul and Peephole, who were still standing in the parking lot of Butter Baby's, staring up at me. "I'm going in after her! If she comes out the front . . ."

"We'll tackle her!" Peephole yelled, shocking both Paul and me. But I didn't have time to reflect on Peephole's sudden burst of bravery, because I heard the metallic creaking of a door opening and closing from down inside the milkshake.

I dipped my head into the darkness below and saw a ladder leading down the side wall of the massive cup to the circular floor. I gripped it and began climbing. After a few steps, I got impatient and jumped. I fell for a little longer than I'd expected, but I landed on my feet, with a great clanging noise. The room was dark, with the open hatch in the ceiling providing the only light. Next to my feet, I glimpsed Tania's flashlight. I swooped it up and snapped it on, swinging its beam across the room. There was no sign of Tania, but on the wall was taped the same map of Bellwood that we'd found in Munchaus's shoe. And there, on the floor, were several Bozo bar wrappers. I was right—they *were* for her. Tania must have moved her control room as soon as she figured out we'd infiltrated the shoe.

I swept the flashlight beam across the floor. There, on the other side of the room, was another door handle sticking up. I dropped the flashlight, bounded over, and pulled on it. The door groaned heavily, and it took all my might to lift it. Below, I saw another stepladder, leading down to what looked like a storage room. I hopped onto the ladder and slid down the rails, and just as my feet hit the floor, I heard a door on the other side of the room click shut.

"Tania!" I called, sprinting for the door. "You can't escape!" My voice sounded fierce, but a creeping doubt entered my head. *What if she* does *escape?* If we didn't catch her red-handed with the crow, she'd slip away with the evidence, and then it would be our word against hers. And would anybody believe a few kids over an adult? Especially if their story was as weird as this?

I flung open the storage room door and swiveled my head to the right, catching sight of the stainless steel counters and rows of blenders and refrigerator doors in Butter Baby's back kitchen, and to the left, where Tania stood at the front entrance, peering at Paul and Peephole outside. She twirled around, ready to race back through the restaurant to the rear door, but froze when she saw me. The robot crow in her hands glared at me with red eyes.

Tania threw one last glance out the front door, then stepped toward me, as if she planned to run past me—or knock me over. I held my ground and gritted my teeth.

"I'm not afraid," I said, and I meant it.

Tania hunkered down like a bull readying to charge. I shifted my balance and glared back. For a moment, I was sure I was going to get my chance to take down a suspect. But then her shoulders relaxed, and she stood up straight. She sighed and shook her head.

"Oh, who am I kidding? There's no point in hiding it anymore," she said in a defeated voice. She looked down at the crow, which she was now cradling in her arms like a newborn. There was a look in her eyes I didn't expect—sadness?

Suddenly, she gazed up at me. "Did you really climb it? The milkshake?"

"Yeah, I did," I said, surprised by the question.

"Wow." She nodded appreciatively. "Why?"

"Because . . . the door was locked, and there was no other way. I had to catch you."

"But weren't you afraid? It's so dangerous."

I started to shake my head, but I stopped myself. "Yes. Actually, I was terrified." There was no point in lying. It was time I broke kayfabe.

"Your turn," I said. "Why?"

Tania Rose tilted her head at me. "Why what?"

"Why this whole thing? The smells. And the sneaky letters to Mr. Nemo and Darrel Sullivan. Why the secret hideout in Munchaus's shoe? And in this big milkshake. Why *that*?" I said, pointing at the robot crow in her hands.

"Isn't it obvious?" she answered, her voice somber. "For New Bellwood. To make Frank's vision of the future come true."

"Frank?"

"Mayor Pilkington."

A sudden banging on the door behind her made her jump. It was Paul and Peephole, peering through the glass doors at us. I started to move, but Tania put up a hand to stop me. She turned and slowly pushed the door open. Paul and Peephole cautiously entered Butter Baby's, keeping their distance from Tania. They crossed the room and stood near me. I could tell they were confused that she had let them in. I was, too.

"So the mayor made you do this?" I asked.

Tania flashed me a horrified look and shook her head. "Frank? Goodness, no. He would never ask me to do anything like this. He didn't know anything about it."

"So this was all your idea?" I asked.

Tania nodded her head slowly. "Nobody loves Bellwood as much as Frank does. He saw a wonderful future ahead for us, and he wanted so badly for it to come true. He wanted New Bellwood to be real. But the mayor . . . he can be a little . . . absentminded. I knew that if New Bellwood was going to happen, he would need a little extra help."

"So you tried to ruin the old restaurants, just so people would go to the new ones?"

Tania frowned and looked at the ceiling. "That wasn't what I wanted to do," she said. "I just wanted people to see how great the new places could be. I wanted the New Bellwood project to turn out just like Frank hoped it would. But it wasn't working out that way. We worked and worked, and then, when the new restaurants opened, nobody wanted to go. They just wanted to stick with their old favorites. I didn't think it was fair."

"But that's the way it is," I said. "People get to choose where they want to eat."

"I know," Tania said. "But these new restaurants . . . they're chains. There are Butter Baby's all over the country."

"We know," Paul said. "But so what?"

"So they don't need Bellwood. But New Bellwood needs them. If nobody went to them, they'd just shut down and leave town. And maybe *all* the new stores would shut down, and New Bellwood would be a huge failure. Bellwood would look like a ghost town, and when they saw the empty storefronts, all the people would blame Mayor Pilkington. He'd never be reelected. His heart would be broken. I didn't want that to happen."

"And that's why you started sabotaging the old restaurants?" Paul asked.

"That wasn't the original plan." She sighed, looking down at her shoes. "It all started with the idea to lure customers to the new restaurants by spraying good smells in the air. That's harmless enough, right? I knew I could create the scents with the right essential oils, and then I came up with the idea of using a drone to spread them all over town."

"But why crows?" I asked.

"Because I figured nobody would look at them twice. I actually got the idea from Mayor Pilkington's stationery. See, there's a little hidden picture in the corner—"

"We know," Paul, Peephole, and I said in unison.

Tania gave us a puzzled look before continuing. "But I didn't know how to build such a gadget."

"So you asked Mr. Nemo to do it," Paul said.

"But why did you have to be so secretive about it?" I asked.

Tania shrugged. "I guess I just didn't want Frank to know. I wanted him to think people loved the new places. That they were going to them because they wanted to. But like I said, the smells just made people crave the old places, like Dr. Dave's. And I got carried away. That was my mistake. If I could go back, I would never have added the stink bombs."

"Don't forget about the rats," Peephole said.

Tania spread her palms out. "What can I say? Once I went down that road, it was hard to turn back. I thought if I could just reroute the customers from Dr. Dave's—just one time—then they'd know how good Butter Baby's was. Well, it worked. And guess what? People started going there. So I tried it again with the pizza restaurant."

"How come you didn't just release the rats yourself? Why drag Darrel Sullivan into it?" I asked.

"I didn't want to get caught," she said flatly. "I'm not proud of that. But if people thought the mayor was somehow behind this, he'd be ruined. And Darrel Sullivan works in the pet store," she said matter-of-factly, "and I knew he'd do just about anything for a few extra dollars. Besides, where else was I going to get fifteen rats?"

I looked over to Paul, whose eyes flicked past Tania to the front doors. I saw what he saw.

"You know, my parents worked hard to start Honest Bratwurst," Paul said. He was staring right at Tania now. "They work hard every day to keep it up and running."

"I'm sure they do," Tania said quietly.

"And Dr. Dave. His ice cream shop has been open for decades. Same thing with Mrs. Lombardi and A Pizza Heaven. Everybody in Bellwood knows them."

Tania nodded.

"I know that new restaurants are going to open up," Paul continued. "That's okay. I know that Bellwood is going to change. And I know that some change is good. But what you did . . . that was a dirty trick. That wasn't fair."

Tania took a deep breath. "You're right."

"I believe you," I said.

Tania looked up at me.

"I believe that you wanted what was best for Bellwood. But Paul's right. Turning your back on the past wasn't going to make New Bellwood better. That isn't what Mayor Pilkington would want."

Tania sighed. "I wish I could explain to everyone that I didn't mean any harm. I wish I could explain myself to Frank."

"Well, I think you're going to get your chance," I said, pointing outside. Tania turned to see Mayor Pilkington, with Elvis on his lap, trying to get down off the handlebars of Dorothea's bike. It wasn't pretty, but finally he managed to get himself and Elvis on their feet.

I crossed the room and pushed open the front doors. Mayor Pilkington, Dorothea, and Elvis walked in.

"Is everything okay, kids?" he said, entering the room in a sweaty rush, still wearing his neon-green wrestling leotard. "I had to get a ride from Dorothea because Tania vanished with the golf cart." He glanced over and saw Tania. "Oh, there you are. What's going on?"

Tania seemed shocked to see him at first. For a

moment, I thought she might clam up and deny everything. But she swallowed hard and looked him in the eye.

"Frank," she said. "There are some things you need to know. About the New Bellwood project."

"Oh?" he said, his face aglow with curiosity.

"Why don't we sit down?" I said, ushering Mayor Pilkington to a table in the corner of the restaurant. When he was seated, I walked toward the kitchen in the back.

"Where are you going?" Paul asked.

"To see if there are any milkshakes," I answered. "For this conversation, we're going to need them."

➤ 17 ⬅

Welcome to New Old Bellwood

For the rest of the week, we kept our eyes on the sky. We saw plenty of crows squawking overhead on their way to perch on a power line or in a crowded tree. But none of their eyes were red, and none of them had that telltale machine-like hum. It seemed like the strange, brief flight of the robot crows was over.

And there were no more mysterious smells tickling the nostrils of curious Bellwoodians—only the familiar soft bite of the early-autumn coolness and the occasional whiff of a backyard bratwurst barbecue. Or, in my house, the odd tang of my dad's homemade tofu.

The chorus of construction hammered on all throughout town as the bulldozers growled and the cement trucks clanged through the streets, wrestling Bellwood into its own future. But despite all the noise, people were beginning to warm up to the changes. The roads were a little smoother and the streetlamps were a little brighter, and the promise of a brand-new library opening its doors soon got everyone excited.

And Mayor Pilkington remained as optimistic and devoted to Bellwood as ever, making his speeches to anyone who would listen. He did have to write them down himself, though, now that Tania Rose was no longer his assistant. After the One and Onlys confronted her at Butter Baby's and she confessed everything to Mayor Pilkington, she'd gone around to Dr. Dave and Mrs. Lombardi and Paul's parents, offering personal apologies for what she'd done. Then, because she could no longer work in the office of the mayor, she began volunteering at the pet store, in their rodent care section. She also started her own business—an idea that she'd had for a long time. Tania Rose's Custom-Made Perfumes was just getting up and running, but she had some recent experience to help her along the way.

Now that the One and Onlys had officially put the Case of the Robot Crow in the "solved" file, I had some time for other things. Like working on Mrs. Espinoza's social studies presentation, due on Monday. I didn't want to wait until the very last minute, so the night before I was set to present, I sat down to put some finishing touches on the project.

My dad poked his head into my room to check on my

progress. "How's the presentation coming? Want to run it by me? Are you nervous?"

"No thanks, Dad," I said. "I'm not nervous at all." And I wasn't. I was one of the only kids I knew who loved presenting in front of the class. Peephole, on the other hand, was probably trying to sew himself to his bed so he wouldn't have to go to school.

"Hey! I've got an idea. How about I come along to your presentation dressed as the Specter! I could demonstrate the Phantom Fling!"

"Thanks," I said, cringing at the thought of my dad hurting himself, or somebody else, during my presentation. "But I think I'll be okay without you."

I did have to admit, though, that the presentation was missing something. I'd spoken to Mr. Patel and my dad, and had done some research on the history of the Bellwood Recreation Center, but I wasn't quite satisfied. The mystery of the Specter was still unsolved.

I suddenly remembered something that Dorothea had mentioned back at the Bellwood Junior Historical Society meeting. She said she regularly looked up old Bellwood newspaper articles on the internet. It was a great way to peek into the past.

I flipped open my computer and logged in to the Bellwood Library website. A few clicks later, I was browsing the historical archives of the *Bellwood Noise*. In the search bar, I typed "June 15, 1962."

A scan of the front page came up. "Wrestling Stars to Entertain Bellwood Tonight" was the top headline, spanning the entire page. Accompanying the article was a slightly blurry black-and-white picture of the Specter himself, leaning against the ropes and holding a finger to his lips. The caption read: "Up-and-coming star the Specter will appear in Bellwood tonight with a touring group of professional wrestlers."

The article quoted several local citizens who were excited about the event, including one youngster who said that the Specter was his hero. "I want to be a shoe salesman when I grow up, but I also want to be a wrestler, just like the Specter," the young Arjun Patel told the reporter.

I flipped to the next day's front page, headed "Star's Sudden Exit Ends Entertaining Night," with a large photograph of the Specter in the ring. Unlike the previous day's, this picture was sharp and clear, showing the Specter's features up close. It was the best image I'd ever seen of him, much better than the fuzzy old videos my dad liked to watch. His face was narrow, almost hawkish, and his bright eyes shone through the holes in his mask. Behind him, the audience was visible in fine detail. *These were the people of old Bellwood*, I thought. They looked like they could be anybody living here now, except for their out-of-date clothes and some slightly goofy hairstyles. There was a guy in mid-yell holding up a hot dog.

The woman next to him was leaning away, embarrassed or annoyed or both. Behind them, a bald man with a mustache and a stern expression watched the action in the ring. My eye caught on his face. Something in his eyes. He looked familiar, like I'd seen him before, but that was unlikely, given that this picture had been taken six decades earlier.

And then I looked back at the Specter, studying his face again. My eyes bounced between the wrestler and the stern man in the audience. Back and forth. And then I realized I *had* seen them before.

I opened the drawer of my desk and rummaged through the mess of random things until I found the card I was looking for. I reached for my phone and dialed the number written on it.

"Hello?" a raspy voice said on the other end of the line.

"This is Shanks," I said.

"Ah, the fearless detective," the voice said. "Did something break?"

"Not exactly. But I do have a favor to ask."

The next day, Mrs. Espinoza held up her hands for the packed room to be quiet. Her social studies class was a little more crowded than usual, with several special visitors standing in the back to watch the day's presentations. Dorothea had invited Mayor Pilkington himself to see her presentation on the Brewster House, and he graciously accepted. Paul had invited his parents and grandparents, and they stood in the back next to Mr. Patel and my own dad, who both came at my request. I wasn't nervous at all, because I had a secret up my sleeve that was sure to get me an A. Peephole, however, was sweating buckets. He didn't like presentations, though his papier-mâché replica of Munchaus's shoe was excellent.

Peephole volunteered to go first, as he always did, preferring to get it over with so he could relax for the rest of class. He presented the history of the unfinished Wolfgang Munchaus statue, giving firsthand details from our visits to the weird monument in the corner of the Bell Woods. When he was done, Peephole scurried back to his seat as Mr. Patel gave him a rollicking ovation. I guess he was a fan of anything having to do with shoes.

Paul talked about the history of Honest Hardware, passing around old photographs of his grandfather and great-grandfather building it and his dad renovating it. As a treat, his parents handed out mini–Swines in Sleeping Bags for the audience. Even Mrs. Espinoza took one, though she said that bribes for grades were technically against the rules.

And then it was Dorothea's turn. In a slideshow, she traced the history of the Brewster House from its origins as a hotel through its conversion into a rooming house for Black people only. She talked about her great-grandfather, the work he did for Bellwood, and the poor living conditions he had to endure at the Brewster House. She described her dream that one day, James Hightower's great-granddaughter would be mayor of the town he'd helped build, and that she would make sure that every Bellwoodian knew about their hometown's past—the good *and* the bad—so that they could make a better future together. When she was done, it was Mayor Pilkington's turn to stand up and applaud.

And finally, I walked to the front of the classroom. "Ladies and gentlemen," I began, "are you ready to ruuuuumble?!"

A roomful of sixth graders gave me the reaction I wanted. A wave of hoots and stomps and whistles greeted me. I grinned. "You might not know this, but there is a mystery that dates back sixty years into Bellwood's past. On the night of June 15, 1962, a legend appeared at the Bellwood Recreation Center for the first time. I'm talking about the Specter, one of the most dynamic professional wrestlers to ever grace the ring. He was on the brink of international fame. The Specter's cat-like athleticism could not be matched. Unfortunately, that night was the Specter's *last* appearance in Bellwood. As a matter of fact, it was the wrestler's last appearance anywhere. He went missing that night, never to be seen again."

I paused dramatically, letting the mystery settle over the audience.

"That is, until today."

This was the part where the fireworks and fog machine would have gone off, but something told me Mrs. Espinoza wouldn't have been cool with that. So I settled for a finger dramatically pointed at the classroom door.

"Citizens of Bellwood, I give you . . . the Specter!"

Every face turned expectantly to the door. For a few seconds, nothing happened, and I had a moment of panic that he had decided not to come. But then the door creaked open, and a bent old man in gray tights and a cape shuffled in. He stood in front of the classroom, peering out through his mask. His stooped back and wrinkled face showed his age, but his eyes shone brightly out at the class. He'd shaved his mustache, but there was still no mistaking who he was.

"Mr. Nemo?" Paul said.

"Is that Mr. Fix-it?" somebody asked.

"*You're* the Specter?" my dad gasped from the back of the room, disbelief in his voice.

There was a moment of silence. And then somebody, I couldn't tell who, let out a little chitter. And then somebody else chortled, and before I knew it, more joined in.

I couldn't believe it. They were *laughing* at him? I was about to let everybody in the room have it when Mr. Nemo raised a single finger to his lips. The Specter's signature gesture. Incredibly, the laughter stopped.

"When I was young, I loved two things in the world," he whispered, his voice even raspier than normal, but somehow more intense. "Wrestling and fixing things. And I was good at them both. But I let one of them go too soon. I still remember that night in Bellwood all those years ago. I looked out into the audience and saw the one person I didn't expect: my dad. I didn't know he was going to be there, and I'm still not sure why he came. Maybe somebody dragged him there. Maybe he came out of curiosity. But when I saw him, I froze. He was the one person that I always wanted to please, but I never could seem to. And he didn't know I was wrestling. He would never have approved of it. It was silly—a building full of people cheering me on, but I only cared about one. I was gripped by fear. I was scared he would recognize me. I was scared he'd know that I'd chosen this as my career path. I was scared that if he found out, he'd never forgive me. So I panicked. I left the ring. I ran out of the building, tore my costume off, and never put it on again. I let my fear win.

"I've lived a good life in Bellwood. I've been happy doing what I love. But I've always regretted the way I ran that night. I've always wondered . . . what if I'd stayed in the ring? What if I hadn't pretended to be something I wasn't?"

Mr. Nemo stopped talking and looked over at me. He winked. I nodded back to him.

He continued: "A wise person once taught me an important lesson. She encouraged me to face my fears. She told me that anything worth doing was going to be a little scary. Well, I'll admit it. This is a little scary for me." Mr. Nemo reached a finger up to adjust his mask, which had sagged down over his eyes a little. "Over the last sixty years, I've fixed just about everything in Bellwood. And now it's time to fix my past."

He stopped talking. The classroom full of people didn't make a peep. Everyone just sat there, staring up at him.

"Phantom Fling," a voice in the back of the room said. It was my dad. He was gazing at Mr. Nemo with awe. "Phantom Fling," he repeated.

"Phantom Fling," Mr. Patel joined in. "Phantom Fling. Phantom Fling! Phantom Fling!"

They got louder, and now Paul joined in, then Peephole, then Mayor Pilkington. Soon every sixth grader in the room was pounding on their desk and chanting at the top of their lungs. Even Mrs. Espinoza had stood up behind her desk and was shouting along.

"Phantom Fling!" we all demanded.

Mr. Nemo stood still, peering out at the class. I thought I detected the hint of a smile appear on his lips. But then he sprang into action. One step to the right. Two to the left. A dip, a swoop, a duck, and then a *lift*!

Maybe it was a little slower than it used to be. Okay, a lot slower—after all, Mr. Nemo was an old man. And maybe it wouldn't have knocked a giant off his feet. But there was no denying it. The Specter still moved like a cat. Like water. The Specter still had it.

The room erupted into applause. Everyone leapt to their feet, clapping like crazy. My dad and Mr. Patel high-fived in the back of the room, both losing their balance at the same time. Mayor Pilkington attempted his own Phantom Fling, but wisely stopped before crashing into any sixth graders. I caught Mrs. Espinoza's eye, and she beamed with approval.

And when I looked to see Mr. Nemo's reaction, the only thing I saw was the door to the classroom gently closing.

He was gone. Vanished. Like a ghost. But this time, I had a feeling the Specter would be back.

⇒ 18 ⇐

A Bright Future

That Monday evening, the Lyrical Warriors decided to take a night off from the ring and meet at Dr. Dave's for an old-fashioned ice cream party. It was Mayor Pilkington who suggested it, and everyone agreed it was a great idea.

But it wasn't just wrestler-poets at the get-together. We also invited Dorothea and Elvis, and Mr. Nemo, who showed up as himself, without a mask or cape.

Curious passersby noticed the party and stopped in for a scoop or two. Harmonica Ed showed up on his bike, trailed as always by Flyin' Brian Saucer. Ed pulled out his instrument and started fuzzing out an upbeat blues shuffle. Paul's parents began dancing to the music. At least, I think they were dancing—Mr. Marconi was wiggling and shaking like an electric eel had slithered down his pants. He kept on urging Peephole's mom and dad to join them, but they just stuck to their no-thank-yous. Trillium, though, was giggling and spitting up and giggling some more. Elvis had been spotted earlier, wearing his invisibility helmet, but now he was nowhere to be seen.

Behind me, Mrs. Newsome and my mom were discussing their favorite poems, and Darrel Sullivan kept saying he didn't know anything about poetry, but he *had* learned a thing or two about giving haircuts to exotic rodents.

Out in the parking lot, Mr. Nemo was trying to teach the Phantom Fling to my dad, but he wasn't exactly picking it right up. He kept losing his footing on the duck and lift, nearly crashing into Jeb and Zeb Beverly, who seemed to be arguing over whose triple-scoop cone was taller.

Next to us, Mayor Pilkington and Dorothea were discussing the wording for a new historical marker to be put up at the Brewster House.

"I think you should give your presentation to the town council," Mayor Pilkington urged. "They should know the history, too. And maybe we can start planning the perfect place for the new Bellwood History Museum."

"I'd love to. How about you come to the Bellwood Junior Historical Society meeting this Saturday and we can work out the details?"

"I didn't know we *had* a junior historical society," Mayor Pilkington said. "I'll come on Saturday, but on one condition."

"What's that?"

"Well, I'm in need of a new assistant. Maybe you could consider spending a few hours a week working in Town Hall. After all, the future mayor of Bellwood should get to know the place a little, don't you think?"

Dorothea smiled and nodded.

"You know," I said to Paul and Peephole, "this town never ceases to surprise me. Two weeks ago, the three of us were right here, waiting in line for some Dr. Dave's ice cream that we never got. And now here we are again."

"Some things are worth waiting for," Paul said. He held his milkshake up in the air. "To Bellwood. Old and New."

I lifted my cup into the air and clinked Paul's.

"And to Dr. Dave," Peephole said, "for making a heck of a milkshake."

A slight movement behind me caught my attention. I turned to see Mr. Nemo smiling at me, holding something wrapped in newspaper.

"If it weren't for you," he began, "I never would have dug my old gray tights out of the closet. I owe you one for being such a good detective." He extended the wrapped object to me.

"What's this?"

"Just something that I've had for many, many years. Actually, I wasn't much older than you when I found it. It's been sitting in my closet for a long time, just like my Specter costume. I figured it was time to pass it on. You can keep it if you like. Or you can pass it on. The choice is yours."

I carefully unwrapped the gift. It was an action figure, and it looked old.

"Is that Superman?" Peephole asked.

"Oh, my . . . ," Paul said.

And then I realized what it was, too. I looked up at Mr. Nemo, amazed. "So this *hasn't* been sitting up in Funston's Oak for all those years?"

"Not a drop of squirrel poop on it," Peephole marveled.

"This is worth a fortune!" I said. "How come you never told anybody about it?"

Mr. Nemo smiled. "What did I tell you? I'm good at keeping a secret." With that, he melted back into the crowd.

Harmonica Ed began playing another tune, and this time it looked like he had company. My dad was next to him, preparing to play his trumpet, which I hadn't even realized he'd brought. But he had mentioned how inspired he was by the Specter's words to my social studies class. My dad was passionate about the trumpet, and even though everybody sort of wanted him to, he wasn't going to give it up.

"New toy?"

I looked down to see Elvis eyeing the Superman action figure with curiosity. Dorothea stood behind him, her eyes wide with recognition.

"Yeah," I said. "New, but also old. Hey, maybe this can go in the Bellwood History Museum. It should have a nice place behind glass. When the museum gets built, of course."

Dorothea smiled.

"And maybe you can hang on to it until then." I handed the figure to Elvis, who nodded a quick thanks and immediately started flying it through the crowd.

I looked back over at the party just in time to see my dad pull his trumpet out of its case. He bobbed his head to Harmonica Ed's song, then raised the instrument to his lips and blew.

Squank!

At the sudden noise, a flock of crows fluttered from the top of the giant milkshake across the street at Butter Baby's. They paused there, hovering, as if they weren't sure which way to go, each one off in its own direction, or as a group in search of a quieter place to perch. *Caw! Caw!* they said to one another. Finally, they all decided at the same time to float back down onto the milkshake, take up their old perches once again, and watch the party. It was Bellwood, after all, and there wasn't much else to do.

Acknowledgments

I'd like first to thank the crows who frequent Lone Fir Cemetery in Portland, Oregon. You inspired this story with your creepy, watchful gazes.

To my dauntless agent, Penelope Burns: your support and insight are unwavering. Having you in my corner has made all the difference.

To my editor, Kelly Delaney: your enthusiasm and passion are infectious, and your guidance made this book infinitely better. Thank you for seeing Bellwood as a real place.

To my parents, family, and friends: I carry your belief and encouragement with me every time I sit down to write.

To Anna: as ever, you moved mountains to give me time to write. Thank you for your love, for your honest edits, and for the incredible amount of work that you do. Your name should be on the cover, too.

And finally, to my readers, young and old: these stories are for you!

About the Author

When he's not teaching high school English and history, rooting for the Cleveland Cavs, or protecting the neighborhood with his two superhero children, DOUG CORNETT likes to curl up with a good mystery. He is also the author of *Finally, Something Mysterious*. He lives in Ohio with his family.

DougCornettWrites.com

Don't miss the One and Onlys
first adventure!